RISE

OF

THE

RED

HAND

JASON LANCOUR

WANDERING BEAR CREATIVE

MAP OF CENTRAL LANKARA

Focusing on territories described within this narrative

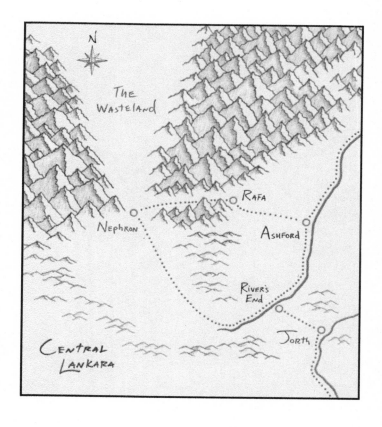

CONTENTS

ACKNOWLEDGEMENTS

This book is set in a world built by many. Though I may have given it voice, it would not be what it is without the contributions of my closest friends; Bob Carter, Bill Kretz, Les Harper, and my brother, Casey Lancour.

Admittedly, it has taken quite some time to go from gaming sessions in Bill's basement in the late 80s to talk of books someday, to eventual manuscripts (constantly alternating between action and long periods of dormancy). I could write a book about the journey of writing my novels, but I feel like I should write the actual novels first.

So, here is the first. I hope you enjoy it.

CHAPTER ONE

Lena glanced around the dimly lit tavern, scanning for the stranger she was supposed to meet. An acquaintance through the Free Blade's Guild had arranged the meeting, and while she had no reason to mistrust the Guild, her new potential employer was well over a half-hour late. She placed her teacup on the table and unconsciously adjusted the fit of the broadsword hanging at her hip.

A serving girl looked across the room at Lena with an inquiring arched eyebrow. Lena was accustomed to second glances from townsfolk in places like this. She was athletically built – as wide across the shoulders and as tall as most men. Her shoulder-length golden hair was tied behind her head in a neat bundle befitting the upcoming business meeting but in stark contrast to the long, loose hairstyles of the women who lived in the smaller, more rural towns along the Raval River. The serving girl inclined her head toward the teapot on Lena's table. She waved the server off for the fourth time. This *was* a business meeting, after all, so the whiskey would have to wait. The man she was looking for was an Ialu – shorter by a head than the average human, though half again as broad across the shoulders.

Pale of skin and completely hairless, the Ialu traditionally adorned themselves generously with tattoos of varying significance. There was a clear and distinct code to an Ialu's tattoos, such that you could tell a lot about someone with a simple glance. Clan and family affiliations were displayed clearly to anyone with the skill to decipher the symbols. Unfortunately, Lena did not possess such skill, nor did many outside of the Ialu race.

It did, however, serve to make her new potential business partner much easier to spot in a crowd. The door swung open briefly, allowing a breath of cool night air to swirl in around her ankles. The figure in the door removed his hood to reveal the tattooed bald scalp she was looking for. He was old. Very old. Definitely her man. He peered around into the shadows of the tavern, stepping politely to one side, lest he block the doors to the tavern with his thick stature. Lena stood and lifted her hand. The man spotted her, split his face into a wide grin, and approached her table.

"Lena Sullivan, I presume?" he asked with a slight bow.

"Indeed," she replied and gestured to the stool across the table. She had specifically requested a stool from the barman, with the understanding that this was the preference of traditional Ialu culture – to be seated at an equivalent height when dealing with non-Ialu.

"As you have surmised, I am Professor Kristaad Durwynn, and I am at your service," he responded as he eased himself onto the stool.

"And I yours," she replied. She had been given a quick tutorial on the traditionally proper way to meet a distinguished Ialu, and judging by the fellow's congenial demeanor as he settled onto the stool, she felt she had gotten it right so far. "Tea?" she offered. He nodded with a gesture, and she poured from the porcelain teapot into his waiting cup. She sat patiently while he swirled and blew into his tea, watching as he took a few tentative sips of the hot beverage, looking around the dark tavern at the other patrons who shared the room. This was a relatively quiet section of a relatively quiet town. She had been through Jorth a few times in recent years, picking up freelance work here and there all along the river basin. The town was nothing exceptional, not much to either like or dislike. It was a crossroads town at a strategic point along the river, nothing more. A place on the way to other places. This particular tavern was a few blocks off the main strip, removed by a comfortable margin from the waterfront and the livelier nightlife accompanying such real estate. The crowd here seemed content to sit and quietly enjoy their food and drink and leave each other alone. She would have to remember this place for future business meetings if and when she would be back in Jorth.

"So," Durwynn began, gently placing his teacup onto the saucer. "As you are aware, I seek to employ the services of a bodyguard. I understand from our friend at the... um..." He wrinkled his forehead. "...The Guild... Free Blades. Yes, that's it. Free Blades Guild." He smiled.

"Jako," Lena provided.

"Yes, Jako. He spoke very highly of you. I am aware of your qualifications. Most impressive." He produced a small journal from the folds of his dark brown robes. Fiddling with the pages for a moment, he found the section he sought. "Pheldian Fighter's Academy. Also, traditional eastern fencing under..." He searched his notes for a moment. "Ah. Master Garis

4

Shelnaav in Pelkin. Well done." He stopped for a moment to sip his tea.

"Thank you, sir," Lena offered.

"You have earned your honors." He tipped his teacup in salute. "I am old," he went on. "Well over five score years... six now!" He paused with a sigh. "These decades have taken their toll upon me. Gone, unfortunately, are the days that I could provide for my own physical safety. In my day, however..." He trailed off, gazing into the empty space between them. Judging by the breadth of his shoulders alone, Lena had no doubt that he was likely a formidable opponent as a younger man. Time robs us all, however. "That being said. I do not wish to have some lumbering, mouth breathing oaf, dogging my heels and distracting me from my work. I want someone capable but subtle," he finished with a glitter in his eye.

"Certainly," Lena offered. "You mentioned your work?"

"Ah. Yes. I am writing a book – history, you see. I am a history professor at the Toctillian Academy of Arts and Sciences." He took another sip from his tea. "I am working on some research for my book, and my travel takes me into places where a fellow might find himself in physical danger. Hence, a bodyguard." He gestured across the table. "Now. To the more important phase of this conversation." His voice took on a serious tone. Here is where we talk about money, Lena thought. She had rehearsed this part.

"My rate..." she began.

"Yes, the rate you had proposed will do nicely." He dismissed the subject with a wave. That was easy, Lena thought. "Most. Importantly. What books have you been reading?" he asked. The serious look had not drifted from his face. Lena had the distinct impression that the success of her interview hinged on the answer.

"I most recently re-read *Military History*, by Dojan G'thar," she stated.

"Ahhh. Very good. Your thoughts?" His face was unreadable, but there was a distinct twinkle in his eye.

"I, of course, acknowledge his expertise and thorough referencing..." she began. Not knowing the professor's position on such a traditional and widely accepted volume of history, she hesitated to share her honest opinion. He cracked the tiniest smile. "To be quite honest though, upon a fresh reading, and seen in the light of a greater volume of life experience than I had when I first read it…"

"Yes. Of course. Go on." He gestured impatiently.

"I feel like his depiction of the battle of Edom is romanticized." She paused to sip her tea and gauge his reaction. The sparkle in his eyes had increased. "Truly, though…" she went on, emboldened. "There is just no way one single man can defend a bridge for that long against that many foes. Of course, we all love the stories of Marjodoc and his stand, but it's more likely he had some help."

"Indeed. Anything else?" He could no longer contain his smile.

"I think G'thar's reasoning behind the breaking of the siege of Delvatha is flawed. I believe his account is as factually accurate as it can be, but his analysis shows bias. We all like to believe that Tolnek won the day through grit and perseverance – by making the hard choices, but I feel the truth is more basic. If the Horde had been at all competent, Tolnek, Delvatha, and any remnant of a civilized people would have been erased. Just look at the numbers."

"Excellent!" He nearly clapped his hands with enthusiasm. "History is written by the winners. There is always bias," he added. "And," he looked over his shoulder and lowered his voice as if about to blaspheme. "I've been to the bridge in Edom. Two wagons can pass each other. It's too wide for one man to hold." He winked. "I have heard enough. The job is yours if you'll take it. Do you have any questions for me first?"

"Where are we going, and when do we start?" she asked with a smile. That he didn't haggle over the rate was encouraging. She had at least expected him to push it back to a daily rate, but her stipulation for a weekly pay interval had gone undisputed.

"I have attached myself to a trade caravan that will eventually arrive in Nephron. Once we arrive in the city, I will no longer require your services. We will depart in the morning."

"Nephron." She hadn't been there before, but Nephron was well known to be a stronghold for nearly all of the Ialu warrior clans – a logical destination for an Ialu historian and a very safe town. Travel to Nephron from Jorth was simple and direct, along a wide, secure road. "I don't want to talk myself out of a job, sir, but why do you need me if you're traveling with a caravan to Nephron?"

"We won't be going straight there. My research takes me first to a small town in the foothills of the eastern mountains there; Rafa. Perhaps you're familiar?" Lena shook her head. "Well, you shall be. We will travel along the Poluvis River until we reach the town of Ashford, then we break north toward Rafa. Once we leave the river, I am afraid your services will be quite valuable, though, I hope, not put to the test."

"Excellent." Lena stood and offered her hand. "My sword is at your service." He took her hand in both of his in a firm grasp.

"Lovely. Now. This tea has been enjoyable, but what say you to a taste of port?" he offered. Ugh. She hesitated for the briefest moment. "Bear in mind that I can't abide dishonesty," he followed.

"Well, sir, I generally don't care for port."

"Excellent. That was your final test. Ghastly stuff, port. Brandy then?" He waved at the serving girl without waiting for an answer.

* * * * *

Lena locked eyes with the woman in front of her, squinting slightly at the glare of the morning sun. The other woman's deep brown, almost black eyes were unreadable as stone, gazing back into Lena's icy blue, nearly grey eyes as she awaited Lena's answer.

"Miss Reyhas, I'm sure you understand that my first priority is the safety of my client," Lena responded.

"And my priority is the safety of my caravan. And you may call me Zahra," the woman responded. "I only need to know if I can count on you or no," Zahra went on. She spoke matter-of-factly, being neither confrontational nor congenial. Zahra was Muradinian; her darkly warm, almost golden-colored skin, her apparent fondness for silk scarves, and the precise way she enunciated her consonants, were clear indicators of her heritage.

"Given that the safety of this caravan is directly related to the safety of my client, if we are attacked, I will fight to defend not only my client but also the caravan as a whole," Lena explained.

"But will you turn and run with your client if you feel the fight is going poorly?" Zahra folded her arms. Lena looked over her shoulder at the aged professor. He had been only a few minutes late that morning and had kept a brisk pace walking through the town to the caravan's muster point, but he now sat on a crate, winded, mopping his brow with a black kerchief.

"I don't think running is my client's strongest tactical option," Lena responded candidly. Zhara smiled and ran a finger along the thin golden chain that connected the ring that pierced her nostril to a ring through her earlobe.

"Hasah!" she shouted.

"Yes, my love," her husband replied as he stepped from behind a nearby wagon.

"It would appear that we are blessed with additional security on our trip," she stated.

"Excellent." He turned to look more closely at Lena, taking in her broadsword and gambeson. "I am happy to extend Miss..."

"Lena. Lena Sullivan."

"Miss Sullivan, a pleasure. I am happy to extend Miss Sullivan a discounted rate for her travel with us in appreciation for her generous offer to provide additional security." Hasah smiled, a wide grin splitting his golden face.

"And I would be happy to provide you and your lovely wife a discounted rate for such services, in kind," Lena replied, smiling.

"Ha!" Hasah laughed, snapping his fingers. "I like this one. I suppose I shall have to charge our other clients extra for the value of having such a sturdy warrior with us and to recuperate my losses for providing our friend Lena with free passage." He threw up his hands as if resigning to his own financial ruin.

"Have all of our client wagons arrived?" Zahra asked.

"All but one."

"I will wait no more than an hour," she stated. "If you will pardon me, Miss Sullivan, I must attend to my wagons. We depart shortly." With a slight incline of her head, she turned away.

"And if we wait at all, I shall charge them an additional ten percent..." Hasah began as the two disappeared into the swirl of activity surrounding the wagon train.

"Muradinians." The professor had made his way to stand beside Lena and watched the couple retreat into the swirl of activity. "A lovely people. Have you been to Muradin?" he asked Lena.

"No, sir."

"Ah. If you have the opportunity, you should see it." He spoke absently as he arranged items on the back of his stout *velni* horse. The shorter stature but still significant breadth of the Ialu people required a mount of compact strength. The velni horse had been bred specifically for Ialish needs. Known more for their sturdy build than for their speed, the velni horse had a reputation both for endurance and the frequency with which they displayed a poor disposition toward the rest of horse-kind. "Beautiful city, Muradin. All stucco and tile. Very warm in the summers. Dry though. The palace of the Raha'jin is one of the most magnificent structures in the world. The Grand Dome... oh, and the gardens!" He trailed off, lost in memory.

"It sounds lovely, sir."

"Bah. Enough with this 'sir' business." He waved his hand.

"That will be a difficult habit to overcome, si..." She caught herself.

"Ha. Make it 'Professor' then. The protocols of academia have forced me to accept at least that."

"As you wish, Professor," Lena responded with a smile. Durwynn focused his gaze past her for a moment.

"Feel free to use the time before we depart to familiarize yourself with the other members of our caravan," he started, rolling up the sleeves of his brown woolen robe as he spoke. "I am going to have a brief chat with my kinsman over there." Lena turned to see a low wagon enclosed in a solid wooden cover. The woodwork was meticulously detailed, such that the structure was much like a tiny house on wheels. A few warrior-clan Ialu milled about the wagon, preparing for its departure. A banner bearing the image of a red handprint on a field of grey hung from a tall pole at the wagon's rear, occasionally catching a breath of the morning's gusty breeze.

The professor raised both arms, palms held outward in a typical Ialu greeting as he approached the wagon. An Ialu returned the salute, and the two began conversing. He seems safe enough with those fellows, she thought, silently appraising the thick steel armor and arsenal of weaponry they carried.

"You must be Lena." A woman spoke beside her. She turned to face the newcomer.

"I am."

"My name is Pevma." The woman extended her hand. Pevma was Selyr. Taller than most human men but typically thin as a rail, the Selyr women were almost exclusively the only gender one would encounter. In traditional Selyrian culture, the dominant gender is female, with women filling nearly every role in society. The males would be expected to stay at home and tend to the children and the household. Lena had observed this stereotype beginning to break down in larger cities such as Pheldi or Toctil, but in more rural towns like Jorth, a Selyrian man out and about without his wife would be quite a scandal.

"A pleasure to meet you, Pevma." Lena received a firm handshake from the other woman as they appraised each other.

"I understand you will be joining us on the security detail." Pevma gestured to a pair of large armed and armored human men several paces away. They busied themselves with the preparation of their horses, securing their baggage and saddles. Each was equipped with rugged, heavy leather armor and a stout, tapered sword. One carried a short, recurved horseman's bow as well. "Those fellows are Kar and Shaab, though to be honest, I have been serving with them on this caravan for nearly two weeks now, and I'm still not sure which is which." She waved her hand dismissively. "Their role is obvious. As you may have guessed, I am versed in the magical arts." Pevma gave a slight flourishing bow, emphasizing her lack of any serious physical weapons. Aside from the small knife that hung from her thin belt, she appeared to be completely unarmed.

Lena was not at all surprised. Selyrian culture was steeped in magic in both culture and practice. Nearly every Selyr she had ever met knew at least one minor spell, regardless of their occupation. That a person might not know any magic at all was an odd concept for many Selyr, and some of the more nationalist factions within Selyr culture viewed other people's unfamiliarity with the subject of magic as a sign of intellectual inferiority. While not all Selyr were mages, and not all mages were Selyr, there was certainly a disproportionate representation of the Selyrian culture within the magical community.

"Standard Magic?" Lena asked. Pevma nodded. "Always good to have a mage on your side." The two began to walk through the wagons toward the front of the caravan. The last wagon had just arrived, bringing the number of wagons to four, including the covered Ialu wagon the professor had noticed earlier. The other three wagons were manned by two or three people each, their purpose centered around the trade of various goods, Lena guessed. "Have you guys had much trouble thus far?" Lena asked.

"Nothing to speak of," Pevma responded. "Zahra runs this wagon train from Toctil to Roth and back, usually stopping in Nephron for a short time." Lena suppressed a smile as Pevma clearly discounted any role Hasah might have in managing the affairs. "She hires the security for the wagons, adding and subtracting client wagons and security personnel as the winds of fortune blow. She and her husband travel in this, and she manages the whole affair." Pevma gestured to a fifth short wagon, more of a cart in reality, that Hasah was preparing to depart. "I came aboard about halfway up from Toctil. We've been traveling on the river road, so there is no real trouble to be had. I feel like we often serve just to protect these waggoneers from each other." Pevma let slip a gentle laugh, her violet-colored eyes sparkling.

"You were in Tern then?" Lena asked. "I heard there was a lot of criminal gang activity there."

"You heard correctly," Pevma said. "Plenty of security work if you've got the tolerance for that sort of environment. I, however, am happy to have that town behind me."

"Almost two weeks from Tern to Jorth? That's not making very good time," Lena observed.

"If the goal were simply to get from one place to another, I would agree. Zahra often stops at small villages along the way, sometimes for a day or more, to conduct trade at the markets. The farmers and craftsmen that provide the goods give her a discount for the convenience of not having to leave home, and she can sell at a profit to the next village for the same reason. It's slow going, but since I am being paid by the day, I am in no hurry."

"The more money she makes with trade, the more she can afford to pay us," Lena added with a wink.

"Very true." Pevma smiled. A shout from the head of the wagon train caught Lena's attention. Zahra was gesturing to the two drivers behind her lead wagon as they began to maneuver their teams into place on the road.

"I should get back to my mount. Nice to meet you, Pevma." Lena headed back to the rear of the convoy to where she and the professor had stationed their mounts. She had roped her stallion, Steel, to a hitching rail by the side of the road alongside the other mounts owned by various caravan members. Steel was well trained and disciplined, with a (relatively) smooth temperament. Still, he was trained for battle, and, being a stallion, he would occasionally form very specific opinions about other horses. She preferred to be around when he was introduced to multiple animals at once to avoid any unpleasant displays of equine politics. As she approached the rear of the wagon train, she saw that the professor was still engaged in conversation with his fellow Ialu, though two others had joined the conversation. One of them, seemingly their leader, was gesturing emphatically, and the others were nodding their heads in agreement. Though Lena was too far away to hear the words, which were likely spoken in Ialish (and thus she wouldn't understand in any case), their body language spoke of a level of aggression that she felt required her attention. She ambled over in a manner she hoped was non-threatening and came up beside her client as the other Ialu took notice of her.

"*Kumo zhi tien kovänmal?*" the lead Ialu asked, gesturing to her.

"This valiant lady is Lena Sullivan," the professor offered, gesturing only a touch grandly. "She will be serving as my *shaalkovik* for this journey," he finished with a smile. "Lena, this is Ortran of the *Servé Ruche* or, in the common speech, The Red Hand."

"I am at your service," Lena acknowledged with an incline of her head.

"I do not see a warrior clan mark." Ortran gestured dismissively.

"Well... clearly," the professor began.

"While I would not call her prowess into question, I do not see such a mark because she is not Ialu," Ortran explained as if speaking to a daft child. He lifted his right arm and held his fist to the sky, turning the inside of his forearm toward the professor. He touched the warrior clan tattoo displayed there. "Ialu protect each other."

"Of course, brother," the professor responded. If he had sensed the other Ialu's hostility, he showed no sign. "I think you would agree that any of our kinsmen who are going to Rafa at *this* time, however, will be doing so for their own reasons. Not to protect an old *kovād* like me, no?" Ortran only snorted in response. The famed politeness of the Ialu people was wearing thin this morning, Lena observed. Just then, a young Ialu emerged from the covered wagon and dropped heavily to the dirt road, his boots kicking up a swirl of brown dust. He was in his mid-teens, Lena guessed, gauging both by his smooth skin and his smaller collection of tattoos and markings. He looked around the caravan with the look of simultaneous awkwardness and self-assuredness that only a boy of such an age can adequately accomplish. He wore no armor, and the only weapon he carried was a short, fat-bladed knife on his belt.

"Maco!" Ortran barked. The young fellow opened his eyes wide. Ortran simply pointed firmly at the wagon and glared. Maco turned and meekly went back through the small door from which he had emerged. The professor shared a silent look with Ortran for a moment.

"Young fellow," the professor observed. "Taking an Initiate with you to the festival? An excellent idea." He lifted both his arms palms outward again and clasped them together in front of his face. "I bid you good day." And with that, the professor turned and walked toward his horse. Lena nodded to Ortran and followed. She held her tongue with professional aplomb. Her job was to keep the professor safe, and she did not feel any of these Red Hand fellows would turn out to be overtly hostile. Unfriendly, it would seem, but that was not a problem she had been hired to address. "Are we ready?" he asked.

"Yes, Professor." She offered him a hand as he heaved himself onto the saddle of his horse. He waved her away and settled comfortably onto his mount. "Our extra baggage was loaded into the second wagon." She gestured toward the front of the caravan as she eased into Steel's saddle. Having learned they would have some additional cargo space on one of the wagons, she had packed her heavy armor into its thick canvas travel sack. The steel plate armor offered excellent protection for more serious combat engagements while still allowing freedom of movement. It was not as massive as the personal fortress each of the Ialu wore, but her thinner stature and choice of fighting techniques favored the ability to move quickly.

Any combat armor, however, was still far more cumbersome than anyone would choose to endure unless they were expecting a fight. Lena would bet ten silver crowns that the Red Hand Ialu soldiers would doff their heavy plate armor before the end of the day. She was not unprotected, though. She wore an ivory-colored padded gambeson and brown leggings of thick but flexible leather – suitable both for extended riding and protective enough in a skirmish. She did not anticipate any attacks before they reached Ashford, and she saw no value in needlessly tiring Steel (or herself) by parading around in unnecessary iron.

"They have my books?" he asked, sitting tall in the saddle, straining to see inside the wagon. "Some of the volumes are irreplaceable."

"Nothing to fear, Professor," she assured him.

"Good. Well, we are off to River's End," he said as he urged his mount forward.

"River's End?" Jorth and River's End were twin towns, sitting on either side of a low ridge of hills. Each sat on the extreme navigable end of a different river. The River Raval flowed south from Jorth to Toctil and the sea. Just over the hills, the Poluvis River flowed north and east from River's End all the way to the Pelkinese coast. Each river made its headwaters in distant, separate mountain chains, but the lay of the land brought them within a day's ride from each other. These two towns owed their existence to this quirk of geography, and the citizens of each town were utterly convinced that theirs was by far the superior location.

"Yes, I understand Mister Hasah has arranged to pick up another wagon there before we turn north along the river to Ashford." Lena now understood Zahra's preference for haste this morning. The distance was certainly achievable in one day, but not if they spent most of it dallying. She heeled Steel to a walk and fell in with the movement of the caravan.

CHAPTER TWO

Lena looked down into the wooden bowl, which until very recently was filled with a lovely stew. She fished out the last morsel of potato as the professor spoke to the serving boy about another flagon of ale. She once again thanked her luck concerning the professor's generosity. When they had arrived at the hotel here in River's End after a pleasant and uneventful day's ride through the hills, she had initially cursed herself for neglecting to address the finer points of their contract.

She always seemed to overlook the incidentals – food, lodging, and expenses. Luckily, Professor Durwynn had immediately waved her coin purse away and purchased her a room of her own, and had freely supplied her with dinner. He also insisted on her joining him in a tankard of ale (or two). He had also tried to convince her that River's End was a haven of safety and the potential for an unprovoked attack was laughably remote. She had relented slightly and joined him at the tavern down the street from their hotel without her armor, but her family broadsword still hung at her hip. She was at work, after all.

The professor took a long pull from his earthenware mug and looked around the tavern with a contented smile. This establishment, *The Dark Horse* by name, was a scant two blocks from the riverfront and had already accumulated a crowd this early in the evening. A Troll sat at the end of the bar working on his second or third bowl of stew, the dim lantern light playing across his nearly seven-foot frame. He looked around the bar with casual disinterest, ignoring the raucous laughter of the humans to either side of him. He was dressed in a silk tunic and cotton breeches, and by the finer cut of his cloth, and the way he absently sniffed his wine before sipping gave Lena the impression that he may be a successful merchant or tradesman. A tribal Troll would be altogether different, but tribal Trolls rarely, if ever, interacted much with human civilization (at least, not many *peaceful* interactions). She turned her attention back to the professor, who was fiddling with a long-stemmed pipe. A leather tobacco pouch sat open on the table.

"You don't mind if I have a little smoke, do you?" he asked.

"Not at all, Professor. Please enjoy." He transferred a bit of flame from the stubby and crooked candle on their table to his pipe with a thin sliver of wood. "Earlier today, you had mentioned a festival," she began.

"Yes, indeed." He took a short puff from his pipe. "Five days from today marks the two hundredth anniversary of the Battle of Rafa. You see, Rafa is a small town, much smaller than River's End or Jorth, so they've only really had one battle. They can call it 'The' battle, and everyone knows which one."

"I see," she answered patiently.

"There will be a relatively large festival there to commemorate the occasion. Rafa will have far more visitors than its two inns can accommodate. I have written ahead to reserve a space for us, but I'm afraid that business being what it is, we may lose our room to someone with a larger coin purse. No matter. I've slept under the stars a good number of times, and I would suspect you are no stranger to such accommodations either." He paused to pull from his pipe. "It should be quite the event. Ialu from all around gathered to celebrate their victory. You shall be able to sample a fair bit of fine Ialish cuisine. If you've never had a proper *chokuzen,* then you are in for a treat."

"I'm afraid I'm not familiar with the history, or the... chokk..."

"*Chokuzen.* It's a – sort of – a goat sausage. Properly made, it's a little bit of heaven." Lena nodded. She had eaten some Ialish dishes before. They tended to be meat-heavy and dense with savory herbs, often a touch spicy. She would undoubtedly try the *chokuzen* if she had the chance. "Yes, but the history! Where are my manners? My research pertains specifically to this battle and its historical significance. You see, it was at this battle that the brothers Uzich and Koldûr Skofkaal defended the town, along with their Ialu brethren, against a host of Goblins from the surrounding mountains.

At this battle, they earned a place among the warrior clans and founded the *Servé Ruche* or, as you have learned today, the Clan of the Red Hand. They are the newest of the Ialu warrior clans, and great men of the Red Hand will be flocking to Rafa in large numbers for such a momentous occasion." He paused to accept the two tankards of ale from the serving boy with a word of gratitude. "You were introduced to some of their number just this morning if you recall."

"I do," she answered. "I couldn't help but notice, though that they did not quite appear to be in a festive mood," she observed. "Oh, I couldn't," she responded to the ale placed on the table in front of her.

"Nonsense, my dear." The professor waved his hand. "The ale here is outstanding. We wouldn't want to insult our host, would we?" he asked. She conceded that the quality of the ale was difficult to dispute. "Ortran and his fellows are just military men. They are easily frustrated by delays. I wouldn't read much into it." He took an exaggerated pull from his tankard and spent an overlong moment looking around the tavern innocently.

"Of course," she responded. Whatever politics governed interpersonal interaction amongst the Ialu were none of her concern. Her job was to deliver the professor to the city of Nephron safely. Speaking of such. "I imagine Goblins can count to two hundred also. They may be unhappy with such a celebration of their defeat. Should we expect trouble?"

"I don't think the town will be in any danger," the professor answered. "There will be a large number of warriors there, far more than were present at the original battle. Also, Rafa has a log palisade wall. The town will be safer than it has ever been."

"What of the areas outside of town?" she asked.

"It's possible that we may encounter difficulties," the professor admitted. "I agree with your thought that the hostility between Goblins and the town will be high around this time. In the years since there have been no additional conflicts, but as you are aware, Goblin society has had nearly continual trouble with most other peoples of the world. One of my associates at the Academy, Professor Etokah, is working on a thesis. He's a C'thûn – Velkasian – he was born deep in the mountains there, near Kannoc, do you know the area?" She nodded.

"I once visited Kannoc as a child," she responded.

"Long way to travel for a child," he observed. "Do you perhaps have some Velkasian heritage?"

"I do. My mother's side," Lena answered.

"Ah. Thus, the eye color and golden hair." He nodded. "Well, Professor Etokah's village existed quite peacefully in the mountains there alongside a neighboring Goblin tribe. That's not uncommon, he tells me." Lena arched an eyebrow. She had grown up with stories of Goblin atrocities, as had nearly everyone else; tales of Goblins attacking villages and farmhouses, burning and killing wantonly, stories rife with murder, kidnappings, and thievery. Lena would freely concede that in all likelihood, the actual facts behind such reports had been exaggerated, or in some cases, Goblins had been substituted in for another foe. Probably, many of the stories themselves had been wholly invented or simply a new version of an old myth. However, most stories, no matter how distorted, contained grains of truth. She had heard first-hand accounts from associates whom she trusted implicitly of Goblin encounters that would chill the blood of the most staunch-hearted. Also, this Battle of Rafa seemed to be a well-established historical fact. It was simply well known and accepted that Goblin society just did not mix with the rest of the world.

"I believe it's true," Durwynn attested. "Professor Etokah's thesis will attempt to explore the historical foundations of the current animosity between our society and the race of Goblins. His hypothesis is that neither Goblins nor Goblin society is inherently evil or malicious and that the tensions between our peoples are a result of centuries of competition for resources, and misunderstandings."

"That's nonsense," came a voice from the neighboring table. Lena turned to assess the speaker. A man turned to face their table, glaring at the professor with his one good eye. The other had been lost in some terrible injury which left a thick white scar running from his forehead, through his ruined eye, and down his cheek to his stubble-crusted jaw. He banged his clay mug onto his table, sloshing ale across his sleeve as he shook an angry finger at the professor. "Goblins are as dark and vile as they come," he spat.

"Of course, my good man, there have been many…" the professor began.

"You're an Ialu. You should know better." The man stood and pushed his chair aside. "Take a look at my face. Look at it!" He leaned forward, craning his neck toward where the professor sat, his jaw clenched. "Goblins did this. They did this when they killed my son!"

Lena stood. "Sir," she began. She extended her right hand in a calming gesture but kept her left on the hilt of her broadsword. The man turned to her, fire burning in his eyes. "We are sorry for your loss." She looked him up and down, assessing his threat potential. He was older, perhaps fifty, and it seemed the weight of his years and a hard life had worn him down. His arms were bony, marked with age spots, and trembled slightly.

He was no taller than Lena, and if he weighed any more than she did, it was not by much. He appeared unarmed. She was quite confident she could overcome him if it came to blows, but she truly hoped that it wouldn't. The law in small towns such as River's End rarely cared who started a fight. Both parties would typically spend the night in jail as an incentive to solve their differences peacefully in the future. Lena did not at all cherish the prospect of a night in the care of the local sheriff.

"Nothing that is said here tonight, one way or another, is going to remedy that," she continued. Her eyes flicked around the bar as a habit, searching for additional threats. Her new and rather angry conversational partner may have friends with similar feelings about Goblins. A few of the bar's patrons had taken notice of the exchange and looked on with a mixture of irritation, amusement, or mild interest. One man, in particular, seemed alarmed at the exchange and had risen to his feet from where he sat across the room at the bar. At first, she took him for a security man for the tavern – he had the physical build and displayed an appropriate level of attention to their conflict. As she completed her survey of the tavern, she noticed another large fellow by the door. He also took a clear interest in the escalating conflict and began making his way decisively across the floor toward their table, with an expression of stark disapproval on his face.

"I have no love for Goblins either, sir, but this…" She gestured to his clenched fists. "This isn't worth it." The one-eyed man relaxed a touch. "What is your name, sir?" she asked.

"Repka," he answered, sparing an incendiary look for the professor, who wisely chose to remain silent. Lena looked at the approaching security man and turned her extended palm toward him for a moment, asking for patience. The bouncer halted his approach and folded his arms, arching an eyebrow. The other fellow she had noticed by the bar remained in place. Maybe he wasn't an employee here after all.

"Repka. I am Lena. I won't tell you what you should do, Repka, but I ask you, sir if any of this is worth the trouble." Most of the other patrons had begun to lose interest and were turning away. Some of the tension drained from the room. Repka stared at the two of them for a moment longer.

"Definitely not worth it," he mumbled. "Not worth a damn thing, this one." He gestured to the professor and took a step backward, turning his head to look around. He saw the security man standing a few paces off with his massive arms folded in irritation. The professor brought his palms together and took a breath as if to speak, but Lena silenced him with a stern look. Repka turned on his heel, began to walk toward the door, being escorted most of the way out by the tavern's security man. After seeing Repka to the street, the bouncer resumed his place on a tall stool by the door but not before sparing Lena one last hard look as she resumed her seat. The large anxious fellow by the bar had taken his seat as well and was clearly the last person in the tavern still interested in the previous exchange. He made no secret of his scrutiny and continued his observation of the two of them, well after Lena had given him a questioning look from across the room. He slowly turned away, and Lena turned back to the professor.

"Thank you, my dear," he offered with a sigh.

"No thanks necessary, sir. Just performing my duties." She scanned the tavern once again, making momentary eye contact with the merchant Troll at the end of the bar. He raised his wine glass in silent salute and looked away as he sipped from it. "Perhaps, Professor, it would behoove us to keep controversial opinions under a tighter rein while we are in these small towns," she offered. Lena tried to keep the irritation out of her voice. While she would not specifically blame the professor for the near altercation, a more guarded tongue would have prevented any issue in the first place. She would have to keep an eye on this old fellow.

She took a sip from her ale, hoping to portray to anyone else who might be watching that all concern was gone. She also needed to nip this 'my dear' business in the bud before it becomes a habit for the old man.

CHAPTER THREE

"Pevma." Lena beckoned to the Selyrian woman from across the back of the parked wagon. "Don't be obvious about it, but in the next moment or two, take a look at that guy over by the tomato cart." Lena tilted her head toward the center of the village market. Pevma casually lifted her pack from the bed of the wagon and set it on the ground next to her, leaning back and stretching. She looked around the marketplace.

"The fellow with the grey jacket?" Pevma asked. Lena nodded. "What of him?'

"I saw him in the tavern last night in River's End," Lena answered. "He gave me a weird vibe."

"Weird how?"

"I don't know. It's just a feeling." Lena shook her head, deliberately avoiding looking in the man's direction. "Last night, the professor had a bit of ale in him and was 'professing' a little too loud. A local with different opinions took offense and needed a talking to." Pevma raised an amused eyebrow. "No trouble really, but that fellow over there..." Lena tilted her head toward the man in question. "He seemed... unusually interested. Stared us down pretty hard, and now he's here." Pevma ventured another survey of the man. He was dressed in simple cotton and did not appear to be carrying any obvious weaponry. A light grey, knee-length jacket was draped over his shoulders, making it difficult to tell if he was armed with anything smaller than a sword. He had a cloth sack in one hand and was surveying a pile of tomatoes with intense interest.

"I don't know if it's all that odd. There are few roads out of River's End. If he isn't headed to Nephron or Jorth, he'd be here." Pevma shrugged. "Maybe he's just a traveler who has difficulty minding his own business. He just needs a proper woman to set him straight." Pevma dismissed him with a wave. "But still, if your instincts suggest he might be a problem..." Lena looked around the crowded market. Their caravan had ridden out in the morning, and after traveling at a leisurely pace for most of the day, they stopped in this small village late in the afternoon. Mister and Missus Reyhas had halted the wagon train along the edge of the village's open-air marketplace and immediately opened the wagons for a bit of brisk trade. Lena had noticed the grey jacketed fellow lurking about not long after they had stopped, and while he had made no indication that he recognized her from the previous night, he seemed to be lingering close by for longer than casual shopping required.

"Maybe I'm overthinking," Lena conceded.

"I can set him on fire if you like," Pevma offered casually. "He'd never know it was me." Pevma fiddled her fingers in the air in front of her face, mimicking the casting of a spell. Lena shot a sideways look at the other woman.

"You're joking, right?"

"Either way," Pevma replied with a shrug. Lena looked around the open space at the edge of this village for the professor. He had announced his intention to buy some fruit and seemed determined to succeed in his quest despite any obstacle.

"I must look after my charge," Lena said, hefting her pack onto her shoulders. "Hopefully, I'll find him before he causes any more trouble."

"I will keep an eye on this character." Pevma nodded toward the man. "If he follows you, I won't be far behind him."

"Thanks, Pevma. It's probably nothing." Lena smiled at the Selyr as she walked into the marketplace searching for the professor. She found him only a moment or two later with a sack of apples in one hand and a lovely butternut squash in the other. "I thought you said you were looking for fruit," she observed with a smile.

"Technically, squash *is* a fruit," he responded. "And this little dear was too gorgeous; I couldn't pass her up." He hefted the squash for emphasis. Lena did not entirely agree with the professor's produce classification system, but in the interest of client relations, she chose to let that subject drop.

"Her?" Lena asked, despite herself.

"Well, a fruit is the seed-nurturing body of the plant, so yes, I suppose, 'her' is accurate." He looked at the squash. "I suppose a carrot could be a 'him,' that's a root…"

"Okay, we're done." She suppressed a smile as she offered a hand with the sack of apples. The professor permitted the assistance and went on to chat idly about his love of fresh air, fresh produce, and fresh ale as they strolled through the market. After a few more impulse purchases, they found themselves at the village inn, and shortly after securing lodging, Lena and the professor found themselves across town at the village's only tavern.

For the last hour, Lena had debated internally whether she should mention the stranger that had sparked her earlier concern. As the night progressed and she saw no sign of the fellow, she began to feel more relaxed. Her sense of ease was certainly *not*, however, a result of having a pint or two of ale. As a bodyguard, it was essential to connect with a charge and build a bond of trust. Having a pint of ale was a way to connect. Without trust, a client might hesitate to follow critical instructions in the event of a crisis. The fact that the ale here was rather good was beside the point.

As they stood to exit, the professor left a handsome pile of coinage on the table to cover their meal and showered the serving staff with eloquent praise. Tonight's outing felt a bit extravagant, as did his renting two rooms in the inn for the evening.

Most of the caravan personnel had camped beside the wagons, which seemed at least as safe (if not safer) than staying at the inn. The weather was perfectly pleasant tonight, and the wagons were all corralled in together in a grassy clearing between the village and the river. But the professor was certainly welcome to spend his own coin however he wished. Lena was not one to shun a hot meal and a soft bed on someone else's tab. It did, however, lead Lena to question how much a professor's salary might be (and suggest that she had perhaps taken into the wrong line of work herself.)

As they stepped out into the cool night air, Lena instinctively scanned the street for trouble. She had worked as a bodyguard once before, but personal security was not the sort of job she found to be instinctive just yet. She hoped she was not overdoing it. A few people milled about the street; none appeared threatening. Instead of following Lena out into the street, the professor immediately turned to cut between the tavern and the adjacent building. He muttered something about taking a shortcut and was still fumbling about his belt with his coin purse as he rounded the corner and entered the narrow lane. Lena hastened her pace to catch up with him and began composing a polite suggestion for a route that didn't involve travel through any dark alleys.

She heard the movement first. The quick scuff of a boot on the flagstone from the shadow behind her gave just enough warning to react on instinct. A body slammed into her from behind as she ducked and rolled away from the attack, stumbling into a trash barrel as a punch rolled off the side of her head. As she staggered to regain her footing, rough hands grabbed her by the collar and belt and shoved her face-first toward the brick wall of the tavern. She shot her arms forward, catching herself and bracing against her attacker's attempt to slam her head against the wall. For a moment, they struggled. Lena's opponent had shifted his grip to the back of her neck, and with his arm braced across her back, he was pushing her toward the wall, hoping to pin her face against the brick.

She turned, releasing with her right arm, and spun halfway toward her attacker as her right shoulder slammed into the wall. She lifted her left elbow up and around in a large circle, throwing her opponent's grip loose, and she turned to face her attacker. She fired a hard, right hook into the man's midsection as he stumbled to regain his balance, and while flatfooted and with her back mostly against the wall, she was still able to strike with enough force to solicit a grunt from her attacker.

She dropped her hands to the hilt of her sword as the man regained his footing. He lunged forward to seize her sword arm with both hands as she cleared only a foot of steel. As he drove forward to press her back against the wall, she caught the first glimpse of his face through the heavy shadow. Unsurprisingly, she recognized him as the fellow who had drawn her suspicion earlier that day. He pressed forward to immobilize her weapon, clamping down with both hands onto her right forearm and pushing her harder into the brick.

Lena shot her left hand up and seized the man by the throat, and just as she gained a grip on his trachea, he released his grip with his right hand, lifting to grapple with her left as she applied pressure to his throat. As he unconsciously rocked his weight backward to fend off her choke, she pulled another six inches of blade free from her scabbard, twisting to her right to divert his forward energy into the wall.

The man suddenly reversed his tactics and pulled Lena by the arms away from the wall, using the direction of her force to his advantage, and threw her clumsily across the alley into a motley assortment of empty crates. She took two stumbling steps forward, managing to only fall to one knee. She spun to face her opponent and leaned right into the heel of his boot as he kicked in a stomping motion toward her face. The spacing was awkward, and she was able to turn her face away and tuck her head slightly behind her shoulder, receiving the brunt of the force on the side of her head. She bent with the strike, allowing her body to roll away instead of taking the impact full on.

As she tumbled into the crates, the man turned away from her to face the professor, mistaking her fall for defeat. Durwynn had dropped his coin purse in surprise as the attack began and now stood a pace behind it with his fists raised in defense. The man took a step toward the professor, rolling his shoulders and balling his own hands into fists.

"Take the money, sir!" Durwynn insisted. "It's not worth anyone getting hurt over." He gestured to the sack of coin in easy reach on the flagstones between them. For a moment, the man hesitated. Durwynn dropped his guard slightly and gestured to the purse imploringly. The man lunged forward and seized the professor by the lapels of his robe with his left, rearing back with his right in preparation to pummel the elderly Ialu. He stumbled hard as Lena clanged the flat of her broadsword against the top of his head as if driving a nail. The professor stepped back and watched the man stagger wildly as Lena kicked him in the hip, pushing him to the ground. Just as the assailant crashed on his back to the flagstones, he found the tip of Lena's broadsword beneath his chin before he could regain his breath.

"You're done," she said through gritted teeth. "If I see you again, you're dead." She watched coolly as the man scrambled to his feet and disappeared into the night.

"My goodness! Are you all right, my dear?" the professor asked as he smoothed the front of his robes far beyond what was necessary.

"I'm fine, Professor," she answered. "And I might ask that we refrain from shortcuts such as this in the future." She eased her sword back into its scabbard and retrieved the professor's coin purse from the flagstones.

"You're quite certain that you are uninjured?" he asked as they stepped back onto the main street.

"My mom hits harder than that guy," she responded, panning her gaze around the street, searching for further trouble. "Oh, and Professor…" she began.

"Yes?"

"I respectfully request that you do not refer to me as 'dear.'"

"Yes, of course," he replied. "My apologies. Old men have old habits." As they navigated slowly through the quiet streets of the small town, Lena took one or two unnecessary turns, just in case they were being followed. Once she was confident that they were alone, she chose a more direct path back in the direction of the inn.

"Sad to see the state of thievery these days," she commented. "That fellow could have easily taken the coin and ran. Instead, it seemed he had something to prove." She examined the professor out of the corner of her eye to gauge his reaction.

"I would imagine he learned a valuable lesson about turning his back on an opponent as well," the professor added with a chuckle, changing the subject.

"Professor, I feel I must divulge to you that I recognized our assailant." Lena stopped at the foot of the short stairs leading to the front deck of the inn.

"Oh?"

"He was at the Dark Horse Tavern in River's End during your... sociology discussion concerning Goblins," she began. "I saw him again in the market this morning." The professor stopped for a moment and rubbed his chin.

"Perhaps he also had strong feelings on the subject of Goblins, and only this evening found an opportunity to express his opinion."

"Perhaps," she conceded. "And in any case, I would suggest as we move forward, to avoid obvious displays of coinage."

"Indeed," Durwynn agreed. "I must again express my gratitude for your professional skill and insight." He bowed his head slightly before turning toward the door to the inn. Lena shook her head as she allowed her suspicions to come to a rest. There was something not quite right about tonight's encounter, but she didn't feel there was enough cause to push the issue further. After seeing the professor safely to his room, Lena made a final circuit around the mostly quiet inn, looking for any signs of further trouble. Though satisfied that the day's troubles were behind them, she nonetheless slept in her clothes that night, keeping her sword handy. Something was definitely amiss.

CHAPTER FOUR

Lena took another bite from the small loaf of bread she had bought this morning and chased it down with a wedge of mild cheese. She looked around at the bustling market in Ashford's center square and idly enjoyed the day, keeping one eye on her charge as he meandered amongst the booths and tables set up throughout the square. From where she sat perched on the top step of the stone stairs that encircled the small fountain at the center of the square, she could survey nearly the entire market at once.

The trip to Ashford had been uneventful. They arrived at dusk and, after fielding a non-stop stream of questions from excited townsfolk, Zahra called for the wagon train to camp just outside of the town for the night. As it turned out, today was a major market event for the town, and another caravan traveling south had arrived the day before yesterday. This morning Hasah had gathered the wagons and guided his clients who were interested in trade into the open square here in the town's center. Ashford was much larger than any of the small villages they had passed through along the way; nearly the size of River's End, though, between the two caravans and the resident merchants, the square was packed to capacity.

Lena had spent a part of the early morning in the field beside their camp rehearsing a section of a sword form that she had learned in the Pheldian Academy. She was irritated that the thug in the alley last night had gotten the drop on her, and she worked her ire out in sweat that morning, as the professor slept in late. The previous night Professor Durwynn was content to stay within the circle of wagons, much to Lena's preference. However, as it turned out, one of the security men (Shaab? Or was it Kar?) fancied himself a crack shot with a bow. Lena rather inadvertently found herself involved in an impromptu archery competition last night and was able to defeat the fellow in two closely contested rounds out of three.

He was a rather good sport about the affair and was happy to sponsor a skin of red wine in honor of her victory. She had shared the wine with Pevma, Professor Durwynn, and Shaab (it was probably Shaab), and the professor seemed to enjoy himself immensely – so much that his late rising was of no surprise to anyone. Once the professor had risen and was engaged with the day, Lena had spent the rest of the morning following him around the square until she had retired to her perch beside the fountain. She was currently listening to a young boy who had been traveling with her caravan as he spoke to his father. The two were engaged with selling their trade goods, and apparently, this was the young lad's first trip into town.

"Father..." the young boy whispered. "That man is sooooo tall!" He impulsively pointed toward a Troll who, like many of his people, easily topped seven feet. The boy quickly brought his hand down for fear of being impolite. The Troll wore clothing made from animal hide and waded through the crowd with a frown as he carried an enormous sack over one browned shoulder.

"He is a Troll. They are large people," the boy's father explained.

"Why does he look so mad?" the lad asked. The Troll's face was twisted in a deep scowl, his brow wrinkled with distaste. His father paused for a moment.

"A long time ago, his king and our king made some bad choices," he responded with a sigh. "A lot of people got hurt."

"But you said it was a long time ago. Why is he still mad?"

"When one people injures another, amends must be made, or the wound remains." His father's voice sounded sad. The boy clearly did not understand, but his puzzlement was washed away suddenly as the next new wonder came into view. Lena listened with quiet amusement as the boy's father patiently explained the seemingly exotic peoples that strode past their cart.

A black and white striped Jaan no taller than the boy himself was happy to allow the lad a closer inspection of his uniquely patterned skin and chatted idly with the boy about his own people for a short while. She enjoyed the boy's innocence and tried to remember what that felt like when everything was new and wonderful in the world. She popped the last bit of cheese in her mouth and watched as the boy tried very hard not to stare at the creature who crouched on his animal-like legs by a stack of crates, only three feet tall and covered with short, brown fur. The furry fellow was examining a pair of brightly glazed earthenware mugs from a nearby vendor, clearly torn as to which one to select.

"Azrak," she whispered to the boy. "His people are called Azrak." The boy turned to her wide-eyed and startled. She smiled reassuringly. "And I think he should buy the blue one," Lena offered. The boy smiled back. After that, she became his encyclopedia. He would point out some unknown person or cultural hallmark, and she would supply the knowledge, occasionally quizzing the boy on previous terms. The boy's father was unable to control his grin as the boy nearly exploded from the excitement of the marketplace.

"And what of that fellow over there, the one with skin as black as coal?" The boy (named Corey, as she had learned) indicated the subject of his interest a few booths away.

"Ah, his people are called C'thûn," Lena supplied. "Depending on where they are from, the C'thûn people are sometimes grey as well, sometimes light grey, sometimes dark. Now this fellow…" she trailed off as she took a closer look. Something about him was familiar. Dark brown bands of thick, hardened leather encircled his torso, and a basket-hilted, slightly curved saber hung on his hip. His back was turned away, but she was certain it was him. "Resaka." She recognized him as he turned his face in their direction.

"Is he your friend?" Corey asked.

"Something like that," she offered.

"You should say hello!" Corey reminded her and turned away to his father to dazzle him with all of his newfound knowledge. Lena took a quick look around the square. Professor Durwynn was standing in line for pastries with several of his Red Hand brethren. Clearly, he was safe from attack for the moment. Lena approached the C'thûn slowly, unsure what he would say.

She had met Resaka in Master Garis' fencing school, and the two had become fast friends. She supposed their friendship was largely because each of them had a life that they were anxious to put well behind them. After completing their studies, they briefly discussed going into business together, but nothing ever became of it. Within a month after completing the program of study, they had both gone their separate ways. Perhaps he was still trying to shake his past as she was. He spared her the burden of the first word as he glanced up from a display of knives and saw her approaching. A moment of shock on his face was quickly replaced by a broad grin.

"Lena!" he nearly shouted. A man beside him looked up sharply, and Resaka turned to him and gestured in her direction.

She closed the distance between them, and before she could speak, she was engulfed in a firm hug.

"Resaka," she started.

"What are you doing here?" he asked, stepping back to look at her. "I thought you were off to Toctil to make your fortune."

"Hello, young lady," the fellow beside Resaka said, offering a hand. "I'm Burkus." Lena shook his hand. He was human, perhaps in his late forties, athletically built, but not overlarge. His keen eyes looked directly into hers as he delivered a firm handshake. Not the handshake of a man who was trying to intimidate or impress, simply a suggestion of confidence that conveyed that he was used to being in command of the affairs that surrounded him.

"Lena Sullivan."

"Very pleased," Burkus followed. "Resaka, why don't you take the afternoon and catch up with your friend. I'm pretty sure I can stay out of trouble today. I've got a meeting at eight at our hotel. I'll see you then."

"The good Mister Burkus is my current employer," Resaka explained as Burkus turned away and faded into the crowded market. "Found myself doing a fair bit of security and bodyguard duty lately, though this has been one of the easiest jobs I've ever had. The man scarcely knows what trouble even is."

"Ha," Lena answered. "I should be so lucky. I'm safeguarding an elderly Ialish history professor, and as easy as that might sound, within three days, we've already been in one fight – almost two."

"Ialish?" Resaka asked but immediately trailed off as they stopped in front of a khave vendor. The dark invigorating brew steamed in an iron pot, stimulating her palate as she caught the scent. As she remembered, Resaka was absolutely fanatical about his khave, and the two had stayed up late many nights drinking the brew discussing philosophy, history, music – anything really. Resaka's eyes grew wide. "I believe it's my turn to buy," he offered. After a quick exchange of coin, she held a small unglazed clay cup of the brew, gently blowing the steam off as she watched Resaka wrestle with just the perfect amount of honey for his own. He had purchased a sizable sack of the roasted seed as well (to no surprise), and the two retired to the stone steps of the fountain to sip the brew.

"Ialish, yes," she continued. "My client is writing a book or something, so we are headed to a festival in Rafa for his research."

"No kidding!" Resaka set his khave on the steps beside him. "We're headed to Rafa also. I wonder..." She cut him off with a quick gesture. Across the square, Burkus was talking with a group of armored Ialu.

"I think there's the answer to the question you were about to ask," she offered. "The fellow your guy is shaking hands with is Ortran. He's traveling with our caravan. He's like a captain or something of a warrior group."

"The Red Hand," Resaka finished. "My guy has some business with them, it seems." Lena watched across the market as the two exchanged a few words and parted ways. Resaka had become entirely absorbed in his khave and was likely compiling an in-depth analysis of its flavor profile. He would likely use the word 'notes,' which is precisely where Lena would disagree. Khave tasted like khave. Either good khave or bad khave, but never 'notes of chocolate and red currant' or any such nonsense. This cup was good – discussion over.

"So..." Lena began. "What have you been up to since... Since I last saw you."

"After Pelkin? I wound up in New Param for a bit."

"Pleasure Island? Really Resaka?" Lena chided.

"I needed a vacation," he dismissed. "And while I was there, I ran into our old friend Bejor," Lena replied with a snort. "Yeah, yeah, he is who he is," Resaka continued. "Bejor had come across a rich little lordling who was obsessed with a fictional treasure that he believed was hidden in the catacombs beneath the city. He hired us to keep him safe and to help him search."

"How did that go?"

"Exactly as you might expect. Our patron paid very well for us to essentially goof around in tunnels and drink too much wine. Eventually, his father found out where all the money was going, and the party was over."

"Of course. His father's objection didn't have anything to do with his son associating with pirates, did it?"

"Smuggler. I was never a pirate," Resaka corrected. "And I was acquitted if you recall. Lack of evidence."

"Indeed."

"Well, that is when I met this Burkus character. I've been working for him ever since. How about you? Did you join the Free Blades yet?"

"Ahh. No. I prefer the independent life," Lena answered. "You?"

"Same. I'm not sure they would have someone of my... background."

"What, a pirate?"

"Smuggler. Alleged." Resaka hid a grin behind his khave. "Jako joined, I hear."

"He did. Recommended me for this job as a matter of fact."

"So, you made it to Toctil? I wasn't sure if you were going to settle down with the cavalry job in Drenn." Resaka took a sip from his khave. "You could have popped in on my dear ol' dad."

"The cavalry thing was fun for a while. Paid well. Just wasn't for me." Lena scanned the market once for the professor. He was happily engaged in deep conversation with a cider salesman. "And I was only in Toctil for a short while. I would have said hello to your father if he didn't hate me."

"I think he likes you more than he likes me." Resaka laughed. Lena silently agreed. "So, looks like we will be traveling together for a while," he stated.

"Looks that way," she answered. Resaka turned away, panning his gaze through the market.

"Is this your guy?" he asked, gesturing across the square as he changed the subject. Lena sat up slightly as Professor Durwynn approached, a few small sacks of market goods in his hands.

"Yep. That's him. I'll introduce you." They stood as the professor came to a stop beside them and gently placed his package on the stone step. "Professor, I would like you to meet my friend and colleague, Resaka Devaash."

"*Kikzhi prava pyozkat ky*," Resaka offered with a bow that was only slightly exaggerated. The professor broke into a wide smile.

"It is nice to meet you too, good sir," Durwynn responded with an equally over-the-top flourish. "Your Ialish is good, my young friend."

"I only know a few phrases. *Votch kalinka doq?*" Resaka added with a wry grin. The professor chuckled.

"It seems you know the basics," Durwynn added with a wink. Lena shook her head and spared an arched eyebrow for her C'thûn friend. "What brings you to Ashford?" the professor asked politely.

"Security work. My employer and I are just in from Delcammar. It seems we will be joining you on your trip to Rafa."

"Delcammar." The professor rubbed his chin in thought. "Interesting."

"Resaka and I were both students under Master Shelnaav in Pelkin," Lena offered.

"Well, it is always a joy to be reunited with old friends. It will be a pleasure to travel with you, Mister Devaash. Say, Lena, I could stand a good night's rest this evening. I was thinking about finding a nice inn. Anything you might recommend, Mister Devaash?"

"We are staying at the Bridgewater Inn. It's lovely."

"Excellent. I shall reserve our rooms. I bid you good day, my *pravkovād*." The professor offered a slight bow and collected his bag, heading off across the market square.

"I should look after this one," Lena offered as she collected herself.

"It's really good to see you again," Resaka said. "I suppose I might see you tonight then?"

"Looks that way," she replied, turning away to catch up with her troublemaking client.

* * * * *

"Are the mines up there even operational anymore?" Lena asked.

"Operational?" Shaab set his ale on the bar. "Definitely. The people of Rafa have been pulling high-quality iron ore out of those mountains for a very long time. There's no telling how deep that vein goes. The Margrave Xedrin has made quite a fortune off of the place."

"Xedrin? The name doesn't sound Ialish," Lena answered.

"Ialish?" Shaab looked confused for a moment. "No, why would he be Ialish? Rafa has been a human town since its founding. The Xedrin family has ruled the northern territories of Toctil for generations."

34

"I suppose I was mistaken. The professor started to tell me the story about the Skofkaal brothers; the reason for the festival."

"Oh." Shaab paused for a moment to look around the public house. With the market in town, there was a brisk bit of business this evening, and while no one in particular seemed to be interested in what two strangers were talking about, Shaab lowered his voice all the same. "Looks like he might have left out a thing or two."

"Indeed," she replied. She shot a quick look across the bar to the table in a dark corner where the professor sat with a pair of townsfolk, quietly conversing amongst themselves. "Do tell."

"Well, originally, Uzich and Koldûr were tradesmen. Mining engineers or something. They got hired to get the iron mine started. Instead of a cash fee, the brothers put in a contract for an interest in the mine itself. Supposed to be open-ended – pass on to their next of kin and so forth."

"You said 'supposed to be' I'm assuming it didn't work out that way?"

"Not exactly. Everything was going well – the mine was a much bigger deal than anyone thought. Not much later, the Goblins attacked in such overwhelming numbers, the people all had to go hide in the mine itself. Rafa got pretty much burnt down, and the humans who owned the other half of the mine got killed. The Ialu working the mine defended the entrances, using their pickaxes, hammers, and shovels as weapons. Whatever they could get their hands on. There are all kinds of stories about it, but it was a terrible fight in any case. Bloody as hell." He looked around the room again, pausing as a warrior clan Ialu strode by with his axe on his belt and shield across his back bearing the symbol of the Red Hand emblazoned across its surface. Shaab nodded politely and lifted his mug, receiving a curt nod in response.

"Sounds rough. I'd imagine a small group could defend the narrow tunnels quite well, though," Lena added, taking a quick pull from her own mug as the Ialu faded into the crowd.

"They sure did, but the Goblins had them seriously outnumbered. The Ialu fought down to the last but managed to kill the Goblin King, and the little beasties ran back into the mountains. Once the dust settled, only the two brothers were left alive."

"Hmm."

"Yeah." Shaab's voice dropped to an almost whisper. "I'd get pounded for even suggesting it, but I'll bet the humans helped a lot, and probably more than two Ialu lived – but that's the story."

"It's a good one, in any case," Lena conceded. "Whatever the actual details, the point being the bravery, tenacity, and sacrifice of the Ialu miners."

"Exactly." Shaab lifted his mug in salute.

"Without wanting to spoil your story, I'm guessing that with only two fellows left, the brothers had trouble with their end of the mining contract."

"You see where this is headed. The brothers went back to Nephron, and as it turns out, the battle gave them the credentials to start up a Warrior Clan of their own."

"The Red Hand."

"Right. So, with getting that started – there's a whole process – the brothers had their hands full. They also were trying to regroup to go back to Rafa with some more of the Craftsman Clan guys… I uh… I forget the name. Iron… worker something. Anyway, it took a while, but by the time they got back, the remaining humans had given the contract to somebody else."

"The Xedrin family?"

"Right."

"I suppose that didn't go over well."

"It did not."

"What was the excuse?"

"Well, the human guy in charge of the place… uh… I forget his name… Doesn't matter. The guy in charge said the brothers had forfeited the contract. Tried to call up some abandonment clause or something."

"I don't imagine that was an acceptable answer."

"Definitely not. The brothers had the legal opinion that they owned the mine in its entirety at that point – last surviving title owners or something. It almost came to blows, and the brothers called in an official Arbiter before it got ugly. They still had those back then."

"Well, Arbiters are still a thing," Lena interjected. "Just not as internationally accepted as they once were."

"Huh. Didn't know that."

"I wouldn't worry yourself. Carry on."

"Right, so the arbiter sided with the humans. Turns out the contracts in those days were sealed with these magic disks. Something about a drop of blood from each party on the page, and the disk seals it all. So, if you've got the disk and the page, you win." Shaab gestured to the barman and then to their near-empty ale mugs. Lena felt that Shaab's grasp of the legal particulars was somewhat lacking, but she got the gist of it.

"The disks are also still a thing," she added. "Nobility use them all the time for official treaties and such."

"Oh. Good to know," Shaab responded. The barman refreshed their ale supply with a nod and a busy half-smile. Shaab dropped a few coins on the bar. "So problem was, the brothers had changed clans, they weren't Craftsman Clan anymore, they were Warrior Clan now, so they didn't have the same disk."

"Oh? What happened to it?"

"When they did the ceremony or something to start up the new clan, they turned the old disk in and got a new one. But of course, the new one wouldn't work on the old contract, and nobody could find the old disk."

"It just got lost?"

"That's the story."

"Quite a story."

"Yeah, so bringing us to the present, we are going to have a lot of work to do in Rafa. The Red Hand Ialu are still kinda sore about the whole thing, even though it's technically the ironworker Ialu who got ripped off."

"Hmm."

"The human miners have been working the place for generations now and feel like it's theirs by right, and that the Ialu just want to steal from them. Once the ale and whiskey start flowing, we're going to see some fighting."

"Like what kind of fighting?"

"Probably fist fights and stuff – I don't know if anybody is going to get killed necessarily, but it's going to get rough. I'm not looking forward to it."

"And here I thought I was going to a great big party."

"Well, there's still some fun to be had, I suppose." He looked into his ale mug. "Food will be good. Whether it's fun or not, though, you might want to think about carrying something a little less lethal." Shaab nodded toward the broadsword hanging from her hip. "I've got this here rib cracker for those kinds of situations." He indicated the arm-length section of hardwood hanging from a loop on his own belt. The leather-wrapped handle showed a fair bit of wear, and there were more than a few dings along its surface. "Allows me to make my point without getting the undertaker involved."

"You might have an idea there, Shaab," Lena admitted. She was not looking forward to extricating the professor from a series of drunken fistfights while he explained the finer points of his unorthodox opinions concerning Goblin society. While she did not relish the idea of carrying additional equipment, Shaab did have a point. The authorities in any town usually had a much softer position on violent conflict resolution if no one was seriously injured.

"There's a woodworker here in Ashford – made this one for me actually. I was going to get one for Kar. I can pick another up for you while I'm there," Shaab offered.

"Thank you, that would be great," Lena answered as she reached for her coin purse.

"Don't worry about it; they're cheap." Shaab tried to wave her coin away.

"Nonsense. I insist." Lena pressed a coin into the other man's hand and silenced his further protests with a stern look. Shaab nodded and stood, draining the last of his ale. Over his shoulder across the bar, Lena saw Resaka making his way through the crowd.

"I'm gonna head back to the camp," Shaab stated. "Pevma asked me if I could take the first night watch, and I apparently need to practice my archery some too," he added with a wink.

"Do you think shooting arrows in the dark with a head full of ale is a good idea?" she asked with a half-smile.

"Probably not," he laughed. "I still want a rematch, though." Shaab smiled and nodded to Resaka as he settled in beside them.

"Hello, Resaka. This is Shaab. He's working security for our caravan."

"Pleased to meet you, sir." The men shook hands. "I'm Resaka. Lena and I are old friends. I'll be traveling with you to Rafa also."

"Great! I suppose I'll be seeing you around then." Shaab turned back to Lena before he left. "Rematch." He turned away and faded into the crowd.

"What is that look for?" Lena asked, crossing her arms. Resaka opened his eyes wide in feigned innocence.

"Look? I... What? Nothing. You are free to schedule your own rematches," he offered.

"You feel you have something to say about my freedoms?" she asked, arching an eyebrow.

"I... uh..." Resaka paused, his mouth partly open. "...I am going to order a drink."

"Good choice."

"You want anything?" Resaka asked as he waved down the bartender. All casual demeanor had returned.

"No thanks, I'm still working." She glanced across the bar at her client. His impromptu conversation partners had departed, and he was making his way back toward the bar. He shook the last remaining droplets out of his personal drinking vessel into the wide opening in the floor of the tavern. As it turned out, the Bridgewater Inn and Public House was aptly named. A small brook snaked its way through town to feed into the Poluvis River, passing directly underneath the inn through a charming mossy brick arched tunnel. A section of the tavern floor opened up to reveal the stream below, the opening protected by a stout-looking wooden fence. The effect was charming, and it gave the place a unique feel. A pair of Selyrian women engrossed in conversation leaned on the rail, ignoring the disdainful looks they had been receiving from the Red Hand Ialu all evening. Lena reminded herself to ask the professor more about the unexplained animosity.

"Your client has a meeting tonight, right?" Lena asked Resaka

"Yeah, I'm supposed to meet him here." Resaka scanned the bar as he took a sip from his whiskey. It would be Velkasian. Resaka wouldn't be caught dead drinking whiskey from anywhere else. "There are exactly two clocks in the entire town, and neither one is here. I don't know how he expects me to know when it is eight-o-clock."

"Mister Devaash." The professor extended a hand in greeting. "Lovely to see you again. This is a splendid place. I am enjoying your recommendation. Thank you indeed."

"*Vlazha radny,*" Resaka replied with a smile.

"Ahh, I like this one," the professor said to Lena. "Excuse me, Mister Devaash, may I examine that pendant you're wearing?"

"Of course." Resaka stood patiently still while the professor briefly studied the small carving hanging from a leather cord around his neck. "The raven is a symbol of wisdom among the C'thûn," Resaka explained as the professor stood back. "When it was time for me to carve my warrior's talisman, I needed all the wisdom I could get." Resaka grinned unconsciously as Lena cleared her throat. "Still could use a little more, though," he added with a wink.

"Warrior's talisman, eh?" Durwynn asked. "The stone, is it obsidian?"

"It's an old tradition. And, yes, obsidian."

"Ah, you see, my people have a similar view of the raven. It is the symbol of my clan, the *Zhovatkov uk Poznost*, or Followers of Knowledge if you prefer. Clan Poznost, for simplicity." The professor pulled back his right sleeve to reveal a tattoo of a raven amongst the patchwork of other symbols and glyphs tattooed along his forearm. "You see, he holds an oak leaf for wisdom and a thorny rose both for the beauty of knowledge and for the pain of losing one's ignorance."

"Resaka, there you are." Burkus emerged from the crowd with a leather satchel slung over his shoulder. "Has anyone else arrived?" he asked.

"Not yet, sir."

"Miss Sullivan." Burkus acknowledged her with a nod.

"Good to see you again, sir," Lena answered. "Allow me to introduce Professor Kirstaad Durwynn of the Clan Poznost."

"At your service, good sir," the professor stated, with a slight bow.

"And I, yours," Burkus answered with both palms extended in the Ialish fashion. "Ah. Ortran." Burkus extended a hand toward the Ialish captain as he approached. The young Ialu initiate, Maco, was trailing behind him, his demeanor alternating between genuine excitement and playing the aloof-sullen-teenager that most young men thought was charming. "Is this the young fellow I've heard so much about?"

"It is," Ortran answered curtly. "Maco, this is Burkus, our business partner." Ortran paused for an awkward moment, then cleared this throat.

"Oh, ah, at your service, sir," Maco finally offered.

"And I yours," Burkus responded with no attempt at all to suppress his grin.

"Professor." Ortran turned toward Durwynn with a frown. "Might I inquire of your presence here?"

"This is a *public* house, is it not?" Durwynn answered, looking around as if he had only just arrived.

"Indeed." Ortran's frown deepened. "Yet it would seem that when I am conducting my business affairs, I often find your esteemed presence entirely too close for mere coincidence. One might be tempted to suspect that your interest in my private matters extends beyond a natural curiosity."

"Well, my good fellow, my current interest is in procuring another ale. Standing beside the bar is the most effective way for me to achieve that goal." The professor gestured disarmingly at the bar beside him with his own engraved pewter vessel. "May I offer any of you a beverage?" he asked innocently.

"Thank you. No," Ortran answered. His frown deepened beyond what Lena suspected was the natural limits of normal anatomy.

"Perhaps another time, Professor," Burkus responded with a charming smile. "I understand we will all be traveling to Rafa together. Plenty of time for ale and stories along the road." He glanced up at the tavern's entrance and ventured a quick wave. "I'm afraid Ortran and I have a bit of business to attend to this evening. Our final business partner has just arrived. I look forward to sharing a fire with you, sir." Burkus offed an Ialu parting gesture, palms extend into both hands clasped. Ortran simply nodded and turned on his heel, grabbing Maco by the front of his expensive tunic, dragging him away.

"Paldor, good to see you. How was the road?" Burkus began as a newcomer approached. A tall, dark-skinned man in a dark brown cloak stepped forward and shook hands with Burkus and then Ortran.

"There have been... developments," Paldor began, glancing furtively around.

"Let's discuss this privately. I've reserved us a room." Burkus gestured to the rear of the tavern and led the others off through a door in the rear wall. Resaka rose to join them but was stopped by a gesture from Burkus. "I'll have you keep an eye on things out here. Thank you, Resaka." Burkus turned into the room and disappeared into the darkened interior. A pair of armored Red Hand Ialu stood stoically in front of the door, hands on weapons, as it closed behind them. Lena watched Resaka's eyes narrow as he observed his client enter the room.

"Curious," was the professor's only comment before turning to the bartender to procure another ale. "Well, Miss Sullivan. Mister Devaash. I intend to take this lovely ale upstairs to my room and have a good night's sleep. I shall see you both in the morning." He hefted his foaming mug and headed toward the stairs, waving aside any of Lena's attempts to see him safely to his room.

"That was interesting," Lena commented as she settled back onto her stool.

"All this drama?" Resaka waved dismissively in the direction of the meeting room. "Hardly."

"I don't know... There is *something* going on." She shook her head. "I wouldn't ask you to violate client confidentiality, but is there anything you can tell me about all this?"

"Why would you care?" Resaka swirled the whiskey in his glass absently. "He's my client, and I don't even care."

"Well, if it ends up affecting the safety of my client, I care."

"Makes sense." He shrugged. "I honestly don't know any specifics, but it seems like the usual 'mystery cargo being taken to mystery locations to meet mysterious people for mysterious reasons' sort of stuff." Resaka settled himself on the stool and leaned on the bar. "He's paying a good rate, and the work is easy, so that's pretty much where my interest ends."

"It's good to see that some things never change," Lena commented with a shake of her head.

Chapter Five

"Resaka, Lena tells me you speak some Ialish," Pevma asked. She pressed her hand to the side of the carafe of mulled wine where it sat beside the fire, checking its temperature.

"I do," he answered. "My father was a merchant in Toctil. His primary business partner was Ialish, and our families spent a good deal of time together. His daughter taught me quite a bit of the Ialish language and culture.

"Is that all she taught you?" Kar asked, grinning lasciviously.

"Ah, sir, you wound me." Resaka placed a hand over his heart in mock injury. Shaab slapped his companion on the arm, either in approval of the joke or to chide his coarse humor.

"Indeed," Pevma continued with only the slightest roll of her eyes. "Not speaking any Ialish myself, I wondered if you could tell anything from the arguing along the road today?" She lifted the carafe and inhaled deeply from its steaming opening.

"I wasn't paying attention," Resaka admitted with a shrug.

"Isn't it your job to pay attention?" Lena asked.

"Well, you must admit, traveling with two wagonloads of heavily armored Ialu warriors has a way of making a lowly bodyguard feel superfluous."

"Super what?" Kar asked.

"Superfluous," Pevma added. "It means unnecessary." She held out the pitcher. "Wine is ready."

"Ah. Right." Kar shrugged, holding out a clay mug.

"I ask because it seemed this Ortran fellow took some issue with a fellow from the new wagon. Lena, your professor ventured an opinion that seemed rather unpopular, as I could gather." Pevma spoke in a smooth, almost bored tone as she filled the mugs and cups offered to her by her companions around the campfire, but Lena suspected the woman was going somewhere with her questions.

"Oh." Resaka blew the steam off his mug. "I dunno. I saw, but I was in the back of the caravan. Couldn't really hear anything."

"You think it was cos'... uh..." Kar gestured vaguely toward Pevma. "...you know... uh..."

"Because I'm Selyrian?" she filled in.

"Kar." Shaab made a questioning gesture, eyebrows raised.

"I'm not saying anything bad about Selyrians. I had a Selyrian girlfriend once…"

"I doubt that," Pevma commented with a chuckle.

"Well. She was half." Kar shrugged. "All I'm saying is that it's no secret that the Red Hand have issues with just about anybody who isn't Ialu. Mostly Selyr."

"Kar. Man. That's enough of that." Shaab looked over his shoulder toward the Ialu wagons.

"It's fine." Pevma dismissed the two men with a wave. Lena arched a questioning eyebrow. "He's right, though. The Red Hand are known for their… nationalist perspectives."

"It's from the big war," Kar added, a look of solemn wisdom on his face.

"What war?" Shaab asked.

"The Apocalypse of D'maldreth," Kar answered in a hushed tone.

"Ah, here we go," Resaka muttered into his wine.

"D'maldreth is a myth, but the war was real." Pevma shot a look at Resaka.

"The dark spirit of the underworld isn't a myth," Kar mumbled.

"Are you talking about the Wasteland, and Hollow Mountain and all that?" Shaab asked. "What's that got to do with Selyr?"

"Yes. The same war." Pevma paused to sip from her wine. "As you know, the war had grown to engulf entire nations and finally came to its final battle in the middle of a wide fertile plain, at the gates of the Ialu stronghold of Kemánmak."

"Hollow Mountain," Kar added.

"Yes, the same." Pevma almost sighed. "And during the war, their enemies had besieged the fortress, and the two sides had fought to a standstill."

"And everybody knows, the Selyrian Empress made a deal with D'maldreth, but he tricked her and released his evil and killed everybody. Her side too," Kar interjected defiantly.

"That's one way to say it." Lena extended a staying gesture to Pevma, who had taken a breath to berate the man. "It's sort of a metaphor. Another way – a more specific way to say it – is that The Alliance of Arcanum, in conjunction with the Selyrian Empire, tried to use the Runestone to destroy the Ialu and end the war, but they lost control."

"Pff. Runestones." Resaka shook his head. Lena glared at him.

"Do you guys mind?" Shaab asked. "Pevma, please continue."

"Lena is correct. The Alliance, which happened to be mostly Selyrian, used the Runestone in an attempt to destroy the Ialu, but the power of the Runestone was too great and the magic too destructive. The blast shattered the Stone and killed everyone and everything within twenty leagues, creating the wasteland." Pevma took a short sip from her wine. "To this day, over two thousand years later, nothing grows in those lands."

"Oh. So, you're saying the Ialu are still mad at the Selyr for that?" Shaab glanced back over his shoulder at the Ialu wagons. A peal of laughter broke out from their campfires.

"Most Ialu have no problem with most Selyr," Pevma responded. "It's just that the Red Hand tends to attract people with a more nationalist view, and they seem to take issue with Imperial Selyr specifically. For that incident, and several other times when they could conveniently blame their problems on someone else."

"Well, we are going to end up in Nephron, right there at the edge of the wasteland," Kar added, rubbing his hands together. "Maybe I'll take a trip out to the center, see if I can find me some Runestones."

"Yeah, good luck with that," Resaka commented. "Two thousand years, and nobody has ever found a thing. If everyone died instantly in one huge blast, then how does anybody know what happened?" His question was met with a puzzled silence from the two men. "Here's what I think. Nobody knows. People made up stories about evil spirits and magical stones to hide from the truth."

"What's the truth then?" Pevma asked with a challenging lift of her eyebrow.

"The only real truth here is that people are stupid." He finished his wine in a gulp. "They start a war so big they can't possibly stop it, and for what? It spirals so far out of control that before long, everything they were fighting over is destroyed, and everyone is dead." They sat quietly for a moment listening to the crackle of the campfire and the sounds of people stirring around their fires surrounding the wagons parked in the large field where they had chosen to make camp.

"Well, aren't you a bucket of sunshine?" Shaab commented. Resaka laughed.

"Seriously though, Kar, don't go off into the wasteland," Lena interjected. "There's nothing out there but the bones of the people who did."

"Yeah. I was just kidding. Besides, I think we've all heard about that Princess of Pheldi who needs rescuing." Kar nudged Shaab, who just shook his head.

"I suppose you've got some insight?" Resaka asked.

"I might need to rescue her from her skirts..." Kar guffawed.

"Kar." Pevma glared at him as he struggled to contain his own razor wit.

"She's probably dead," Lena interjected.

"Whoa. That's dark," Resaka commented.

"Think about it." Lena set her own mug on the ground beside her. "How many years and no ransom demands?"

"Maybe she ran away?" Pevma offered.

"Then she probably doesn't want to be found," Lena answered.

"At least not by Kar," Shaab finished.

"My guess is she's dead," Lena added with a laugh. "The kidnappers probably bungled it, and they've got nothing to ransom. Why else would there be no demands?"

"What's the reward up to now?" Shaab asked.

"Won't matter if she's dead," Resaka admitted. "Naah, that trail is cold. Best stay on this cushy caravan job you've got here. Collect a paycheck just to ride around and see the world. Just gotta whack the occasional troublemaker with your stick along the way. I might get into caravan work, myself."

"Hard to find good khave when you're on the road," Lena interjected.

"Agh. Forget it then." Resaka laughed. "I'll just go back..." He was cut off by a string of angry-sounding voices from the direction of the Ialish wagons. Lena rose to her feet. She listened closely as the argument continued.

"That sounds like my client. I'll just go make sure everything is all right." Lena straightened her gambeson and adjusted her sword belt as she strode into the blackness to cross the short distance between the campfires. As she approached the Ialish wagons, she could make out the professor's voice. He and

Ortran were having strong words in their own language. She sighed. It seemed Durwynn had a natural talent for finding trouble.

"Ho there." An Ialish soldier waved from where he stood guard. He had his feet planted wide and stood with his back straight and hand resting casually on the haft of the heavy war hammer hanging from his belt. Lena nodded in approval. A less professional guard might be tempted to have a seat or at least lean on a tree. This fellow was at the ready the moment she stepped forward.

"Hello," Lena offered. "I think I hear my client. Just coming by to see if the professor is making trouble for you gentlemen," She added with a slightly forced chuckle.

"Ah." The Ialu soldier was with the group that had just joined their caravan. She hadn't caught his name yet. "No trouble at all, miss. *Kovnoka* Vochny at your service."

"And I yours," She responded. "Lena Sullivan. I don't want to interfere in their business, but if I may ask, Kovnoka, do you think I should step in?"

"Begging your pardon, miss, I have been unclear. *Kovnoka* is my rank. Vochny is my name." He clasped his hands in front of his chest, clearly distraught.

"My apologies, Vochny."

"None necessary." He waved away her concern. "You may proceed if you like, Miss Sullivan." Lena nodded in thanks and stepped around the wood-covered wagon into the light of their campfire.

"Excuse me, Professor," Lena announced herself. Durwynn and Ortran were standing beside the second Ialish wagon at the edge of the pool of light created by the fire. Ortran was pointing an angry finger and expressing his displeasure in a string of Ialish speech. He paused to assess Lena.

"I see your guardian angel is here to look after you, Professor," Ortran stated flatly.

"Ah. Lena." The professor waved congenially. "I appreciate your diligence, but I can assure you I am quite safe. The good *Vedok* and I were just discussing a subject of strong passion for us both."

"Indeed." Ortran frowned and crossed his arms. "A subject of a *private* nature." He raised an eyebrow (or at least the part of his face where an eyebrow would be if Ialu were equipped with such things) toward Lena in the outside chance she did not understand his hint.

"Of course, sir. I meant no intrusion." Lena answered smoothly. "And given my poor knowledge of the Ialish tongue, your conversation will remain private. Unless there are other Ialish speakers within a thousand paces from here." She gestured into the dark woods.

"I believe Miss Sullivan makes a fair point, my good man." The professor nodded in her direction and took Ortran by the elbow. "If we expect our discussion to be private, we should conduct it in actual privacy." The professor gestured to the forest.

"Very well." Ortran and the professor stepped away into the darkness, speaking in a more hushed tone. Lena glanced around the campfire. Two other Ialish soldiers were diligently minding their own business sitting on folding camp stools beside the fire. One was hard at work sharpening a fat-bladed knife, and the other attended to the leather stitching on an iron forearm guard. Neither paid her the slightest heed.

Lena felt it prudent at this time to make a short circuit around the caravan's campsite, on the outside chance that the passionate conversation between her traveling companions had attracted any unwelcome attention from the nearby forest. They were approaching Goblin country, and one could never be too careful. If, by chance, her entirely necessary security patrol brought her within hearing distance of the remainder of the conversation – well, that was unavoidable. One must put security first. She eased carefully and quietly across the mossy ground and took place behind a large shrub as Ortran and Durwynn continued their debate in hushed tones.

Ortran picked up his tirade where he had left off and made several angry gestures toward himself and the Ialish wagons, occasionally shaking an accusing finger at the professor. To his credit, Durwynn sat patiently and allowed the rant. When it seemed Ortran had momentarily run out of steam, the professor spoke in a patient, almost friendly tone explaining his perspective and gesturing to his own clasping hand as if describing taking or having possession of something. After a moment, Ortran broke in but was silenced by a raised finger. Durwynn reached into the pocket of his brown robe and produced a small leather-bound volume. He leafed through the pages briefly as Ortran chewed on his own tongue vigorously. The professor handed the book to the Ialish captain and tapped the open page.

Ortran read the offered page, gave a puzzled look to the professor, and reread it. He closed the volume and handed it back with a gesture and a word that could only have meant "So what?" The professor raised a finger with a twinkle in his eye and pulled the collar of his robe aside to display a tattoo just below his left collarbone. Ortran paused. He looked closer, squinting in the low light. His eyes grew wide as whatever point the professor had made registered. The professor smiled, patted the younger soldier on the shoulder, and spoke in a conciliatory tone. Ortran seemed to concede his argument begrudgingly, and the two headed back toward the wagons.

Lena heard a twig snap on the forest floor a few paces behind her. She turned slowly and caught a glimmer of movement in the deep shadow of the forest. Her hand strayed to the hilt of her sword. A figure leaned out of the shadow, revealing himself to be none other than Resaka. She shot him a fierce look and placed a finger across her lips. Neither of them moved until it was clear that the two Ialu had moved away.

"What the hell, Resaka?" she whispered.

"I was checking to see if you needed any help," he whispered back, shrugging in a disarming fashion. She ushered him away from the Ialish camp and back toward their own fire.

"Why would I need any help?" she hissed.

"Clearly, you don't."

"I was on patrol."

"So was I," Resaka offered. "And since neither of us was spying on your boss, it wouldn't be at all inappropriate for me to share anything that I may or may not have overheard." He shrugged just as they were arriving back at their own fire. Lena waited as patiently as she could while Pevma teased them for sneaking off into the woods together. Resaka seemed content to allow the joke to stand uncontested, but his grin faded after seeing the fiery look in Lena's eye. Shaab and Kar had retired to their respective bedrolls, and Pevma was in the midst of preparing her own.

"Have we discussed taking watch?" Lena asked.

"I set up an alarm spell around the entire campsite," Pevma explained. "If anything comes too close, we will all know.

And besides, I believe these Ialish boys will be strutting in circles all night for us in any case. I intend to take advantage and get some rest." She settled into her bedroll and paused. "Do you two need some privacy to... finish catching up?" She winked.

"Ah. No." Lena turned to Resaka. "We can talk more later." He nodded and, with a word of parting, headed off toward his own tent near his client's wagon. Lena caught up with the professor just outside of his canvas tent.

"Miss Sullivan. I trust the camp is secure?" he asked.

"Definitely secure from external threats," she answered.

"Ah. Your concern is noted." He leaned closer and lowered his voice. "I am confident that the *Vedok* Ortran and I have worked out our differences to our mutual satisfaction. No need for concern there."

"I am glad to hear it."

"Yes, the remainder of our journey to Rafa should be smooth, though I strongly suspect it will become quite interesting after we have arrived," he finished with a mischievous wink and slipped quietly inside of his tent with a word of parting.

Interesting indeed, she thought as she set out her bedroll.

Chapter Six

"Miss Sullivan." The professor spoke in a certain tone when he was about to broach a subject of a more serious nature. "If you are interested in learning a touch more about Ialish tattoo lore, this might be a good opportunity." He smiled up at her from the saddle of his stocky mount. Steel was taller than most other horses, and the professor's velni horse was likewise shorter than most.

"Of course, Professor," Lena responded. Any information she could use to understand the swirling mess she was about to step into would be helpful. The more, the better.

"As you may already know, we Ialu all have three primary affiliations. Our family, our tribe, and our clan." He had begun to roll back the sleeves of his robe as he spoke. "You see here on the left arm, the locations of the sigils for family and tribe." He indicated the marks as he spoke. "Family is just that – your immediate family, and as you see here in my case, the family symbol is surrounded by a circle. This means I am of the Direct Line. The firstborn of each family passing this distinction to their firstborn and on down the line."

"I see. The firstborn gets a circle."

"Only if the mother or father is *also* firstborn," he interjected. "In my case, my mother was the firstborn of her father, who was firstborn of his family and so on into our ancestry. Therefore, this family sigil is of *her* family since she is of the Direct Line. Had I been blessed with children, my firstborn would also receive this distinction and pass it to his or her firstborn."

"Ah. I see. The Direct Line, and therefore family name, passes to any firstborn, regardless of gender, or marriage family."

"Indeed. Now, if both parents are first born, then the firstborn child of that union would receive the family name from the parent of matching gender. The next child, regardless of sex, would receive the other family name. Thus, both would have firstborn status."

"And if neither parent is firstborn?"

"Then no child would receive the circle, and the family name that the children would bear is based on tribal standing and other factors. There are rules that govern these situations, but that is not important today. As you can see, this is quite different from the human tradition where the woman would take the family name of the man, regardless of her own heritage, and pass that name to all of her children."

"As a side note, given that I am childless, when I move on to the great beyond, my eldest sibling – my sister – and her firstborn son will both receive the circle and become of the Direct Line."

"I see."

"If I had no siblings, then my mother's next eldest sibling would receive the circle, and the line would pass in that direction."

"It is a little complex."

"It can be, and that is why tribal records are meticulously kept. However, it makes family reunions more enjoyable since less time needs to be dedicated toward explaining yourself, and more time can be spent enjoying ale," he added with a wink.

"Of course." She suppressed a chuckle. She imagined that an Ialish family reunion could take quite a toll on the local supply of wine and ale. "And the tribal symbols; how does this differ from family?"

"Tribal affiliation was originally a simple affair. The tribes were all regional. Anyone who lived within the tribal boundary was of that tribe. With the modern penchant for relocation, it has become a little more complex, but the basis is unchanged. There is a system for determining a family's position within the tribe, and certain families are considered Tribal Founders. If one has Founder status within the tribe, then that symbol is also encircled, and the passing of such circle is handled similarly to what I have already described, though the family name may change, based on the same rules."

"Ah." Lena paused as she processed the new information. She could see how knowing a person's social position at a glance could be helpful. "And what of the clans? That is more occupational, isn't it?"

"Right you are," the professor answered with a twinkle in his eye. "You see here on my right arm the symbols for clan and society."

"Society?"

"Ah, it's an overarching category of similar clans. For example, our friends here of the Red Hand Clan are all in the Society of Warriors. You may have heard of other Ialish warrior clans, such as the Black Hammer and the Fist of the North. They are all within the society of warriors."

"I see."

"When a young Ialu reaches the age of sixteen, they must declare a society. At this point, they become Initiates. Over the next few years, they will take one or more apprenticeships to familiarize themselves with the clans within their chosen society. When an initiate finally Declares for a clan, they will apply for membership and face certain tests, and upon passing, they will be accepted into that clan. This should all happen before they turn twenty."

"Our young friend Maco, I suppose he is an initiate?"

"He is," the professor answered.

"Interesting."

"Beyond those basics, our tattoos are broadly categorized by location. The outer left arm is for family and personal achievements, marriage, children, whatnot. Personal philosophies and beliefs can also be displayed here. The outside of the right arm is for professional accomplishments. Warriors would bear campaign badges, builders would bear marks of their work, and so on. As a member of academia, I have a mark for the three books I have written and similar marks for years spent teaching."

"Honors bestowed by third parties are worn across the head and upper torso for all to see." He leaned forward slightly and indicated a symbol that resembled a crest of some sort on his scalp. "This represents my graduation certificate from my own esteemed university. If you were Ialish, you would display your schooling with the Pheldian Academy and such on your scalp or shoulders. The upper back can also be used for honors and achievements, and anywhere below the heart is a space for your personal expression."

"I am unable to recognize many of the symbols I see," Lena stated. Many of the marks, both on the professor and on his Ialu brethren, seemed little more than abstract collections of lines.

"The traditional Ialish language uses pictograms for words. In modern times you will see Ialish words written out phonetically, but the original written language uses symbols."

"Ah." She nodded. "Very interesting." It seemed to her that the professor had a specific purpose to his spontaneous lecture, though he seemed reticent to reveal his intention. A shout from the front of the caravan drew her attention. A ripple of excitement ran through the column of horses and wagons.

"It seems we have arrived," the professor stated with thinly veiled glee. As the caravan rounded a bend in the forest road, the town of Rafa came into full view. The terrain had been growing increasingly hilly by the hour, and as they approached the log palisade wall, Lena could see the hills rapidly growing steeper beyond the town. The dark silhouette of the mountains in the near distance split the colored sunset sky from the green land below. The town itself was small, though currently, it had swollen to nearly twice its size if one included the ring of wagons, tents, and pavilions that encircled the wall.

The road approaching the single wooden gate that breached the wall was relatively clear from the numerous encampments and the steady stream of traffic, both mounted and afoot, that flowed through the open gate. A pair of harried-looking guardsmen stood off to one side of the opening, hardly sparing anyone a glance. Lena found a touch of sympathy for the men for their dereliction. If they had interaction with even half of the crowd flowing through the gates, the line would have stretched halfway back to Ashford. The professor returned a wave from Ortran as one of his Ialu soldiers spurred ahead of the caravan.

"I see our friend Ortran has improved his disposition somewhat," Lena observed.

"Yes indeed," the professor answered. "I believe he is sending his man ahead to check on our reservations at the inn. It would seem Ortran and a few other Ialish captains will be staying there as well. Possibly our new companion Mister Burkus also."

"Very good," she agreed. In this circumstance, Lena was more than happy to have solid walls between her client and the swirling mass of excitement that surrounded them. Ahead, Zahra was shouting and giving commands to the drivers who had begun to steer their wagons off of the road toward a somewhat unoccupied section of the open field surrounding the town.

"Let us proceed into town. If we get settled in time, we might be able to catch some festivities." The professor's eyes twinkled as he spoke. With a nod, Lena urged Steel forward through the gates. She rode alongside the professor, trailing behind Burkus, Ortran, and another of the Ialish captains. Resaka rode his black mare just ahead, sitting casually in his saddle, though Lena detected some tension in his shoulders as he panned his gaze around the swirling crowd. She had not found a chance to talk with him today about the altercation between the professor and Ortran last night. She had hoped to gain some insight concerning the situation before they arrived in Rafa, but as the day's ride had progressed, Durwynn and Ortran got along rather congenially, even making jokes between them, easing her concern.

The roads through town were somewhat narrow, snaking their way through buildings primarily constructed of timber and rough-cut stone. The hilly landscape added to the winding nature of their path, snaking along the low points on the town's footprint. Lena suspected the buildings were arranged according to the lay of the land directly underneath, rather than adhering to any overarching town-wide plan. A cluster of low stone structures nestled along one slope sat at an odd angle to the block of wooden houses beside them. As they rounded a bend, Lena observed the streets here toward the town's center were cobblestone, and many of the structures were constructed of the same cool grey stone. Iron lanterns were set in groups along posts placed at regular intervals along the street that led them into a cramped feeling town square. A man in dark wool was lighting the last group of lanterns with a long stick as the group reined their mounts to a halt in front of the Stoneheart Inn.

"There they are." Ortran gazed across the square at a large statue atop a short stone dais that occupied the center of the open space. He saw Lena's puzzled look and gestured toward the monument. "Our founding brothers, Uzich and Koldûr Skofkaal." He removed his iron helm and placed it over his heart, as did his fellow Ialish captain.

"Come, Lena, let us look closer." The professor took her hand after they had dismounted and led her across the small courtyard to the base of the statue. The two brothers were depicted standing side by side in somewhat heroic 'striding forth' poses cast from bronze in near twice life-size. The artistry was well done, and the details were well attended – down to the swirls of their clan markings. The professor gestured toward the bronze plaque that adorned the front of the stone dais.

"Let us test your newfound knowledge," he offered with a smile. "As you see here on this inscription, the Brothers were originally of the clan Zelshka Kovik, or People of Iron, before they founded the Red Hand." Lena reviewed the indicated text. "And therefore, as you look upon the statues, you could determine which of the symbols on their arms indicate the Skofkaal family, and which ones were for the Craftsmen Society, and those for the Zelshka Clan." Lena glanced up at the bronze images.

"That would be Skofkaal, and there, for clan and society." Lena indicated the proper symbols engraved on the statue's arms.

"Correct." The professor smiled. "Very good. I suppose that is enough history for today. Shall we go inside and see if we have been outbid for our rooms?" Durwynn gestured back to the inn. Lena caught a glimmer of mischief in his eye. She wasn't sure where the professor was headed with the topic, but as they walked back to the inn, he hummed to himself softly, seeming to be content to let the conversation fade. Just as they reached the short staircase leading to the front deck of the inn, the professor turned to her once again.

"Oh, before I forget. Vedok Ortran has requested my assistance with a business meeting tomorrow. I think we should meet in the lobby a few minutes before nine. I'll take my breakfast and khave at eight in the common room if you care to join me."

"Eight for breakfast. Leave at nine," she responded. "Perfect." She deliberately masked her surprise that Ortran had adjusted his attitude so thoroughly in such a short time.

"Lovely. Let's see to our rooms, and then perhaps some ale," he finished with a wink.

An hour later, in the inn's common room, Lena sipped lightly on her ale and speared the last morsel of chokuzen with her fork. As the professor had promised, it was quite tasty. He sat at a table across the crowded, smoky room deep in conversation with a few fellow Ialu, all from the Poznost Clan as she determined. The crowd here at the Stoneheart was predominantly Ialish with a few humans and the occasional C'thûn. The Ialu largely wore similarly styled shirts with laces along the sleeves, that when undone, would allow a person to display their affiliation sigils clearly. The mood in the room was generally festive, though growing more raucous as the ale began to flow. Of the numerous fistfights Shaab had predicted, Lena saw no sign, but she would imagine the mood out in the street could be considerably more unruly. Resaka sat across from her at the small table they shared by the foot of the stairs that led up to the rented rooms. He was busily finishing off the last remnants of a generous plate of spiced, roasted potatoes, which incidentally were also quite good.

"Something is up," Resaka announced.

"What do you mean?" Lena asked. She had already come to that conclusion but was curious as to his thought process.

"I dunno." Resaka took a sip of his whiskey. "Just a feeling. He glanced over his shoulder for a moment. It was loud enough in the room to cover their conversation, but his caution seemed instinctive. "I never got a chance to tell you what I overheard last night. Between your professor buddy and our friend, the angry Ialu."

"And?"

"I didn't catch all of it. But Durwynn seemed to think there is a connection between Delcammar and whatever Ortran is up to."

"Delcammar? What's that got to do with anything?"

"My boss, Burkus – he and I just came from there. We picked up that tall guy, Paldor, in town before we came down to Ashford."

"Hmm."

"Your professor said Delcammar is the home of the iron men or something. I have no idea what that means, though." Resaka shrugged.

"Zelshka Kovik?" Lena asked.

"Uh, yeah. Iron men." Resaka looked at her questioningly. "You learning Ialish now?"

"It's a clan title. As it turns out, it's also the clan the Skofkaal Brothers were originally from."

"Interesting." Resaka shrugged. "I guess. He also said that Ortran needed him. And now the whole lot of us are going to a meeting tomorrow at City Hall."

"City Hall?" Lena asked. "The professor didn't mention that part."

"Well, I guess we will find out more tomorrow." Resaka shrugged and took another pull from his whiskey. Lena looked around the room. Ortran was seated at a low wide table across from them with several other Ialish captains. They had collected a respectable array of empty mugs and seemed unlikely to slow down anytime soon. She found herself hoping the professor would retire to his room soon before the crowd here grew overly rambunctious. He was deep in an animated conversation with his colleagues and seemed in no hurry to conclude his evening. Lena let out a sigh. Resaka smirked and lifted his head back to the table where Ortran sat. "Something has got him all riled up." Lena turned back to the warriors' table and saw Ortran was struggling to get out of his bench seat past his compatriots. He was waving toward the stairs and gesturing firmly.

"What's his deal?" She turned to look at the stairs behind her. Maco was taking the last step into the room. He, too, was wearing the open-sleeved tunic that seemed popular for these kinds of events. His sleeves were open, and as he swaggered his first few steps into the room, Lena caught a glance at his left forearm. She stifled a gasp.

"Maco!" Ortran closed the distance with angry strides. "We talked about this!" He took his younger companion by the trailing section of unlaced sleeve and all but dragged him back upstairs, glancing warily over his shoulder at the room as they disappeared from view.

"Maybe he is supposed to be grounded." Resaka laughed.

"Did you see his family sigil?" Lena asked quietly.

"Uh… no." Resaka put his glass on the table. "You look pretty serious right now." He glanced around the room quickly. "Are we in trouble?"

"I don't know." Lena studied the faces of the other Ialu in the room, looking for a reaction that would indicate if they saw what she had seen. The rest of the room carried on as they had been – eating, laughing, drinking, and smoking.

"You're kind of freaking me out here," Resaka half-joked.

"That kid." Lena jerked her head in the direction of the stairs. She leaned in across the table. "If I read his tattoo right, he's of the direct line to the Skofkaal family," she almost whispered.

"Say again?" Resaka looked incredulous. "You mean…"

"Yes. I saw the family sigil tonight on the statue as we were riding in."

"Yeah, well, it doesn't *necessarily* mean…" Resaka began but was silenced as Lena waved a finger.

"It was circled. The professor made a point today… very deliberately. I think he was trying to warn me…"

"Ahh, okay, I'm not quite following you right now, but if you're sure that kid is who you say he is, then I believe you." Resaka looked once more around the room.

"Well, I suppose our meeting tomorrow is going to be interesting indeed." Lena relaxed into her chair and finished the last of her ale. She silently decided to attend the meeting with her heavier armor and broadsword, despite Shaab's suggestions.

CHAPTER SEVEN

Lena glanced around the hall of Rafa's single municipal building. There were enough people present at this meeting to warrant the use of the main hall, and after hurriedly ushering out anyone who was not specifically involved with this gathering, the Mayor of Rafa, Latham Harcort, sat impatiently at the head of a dark oak table in the center of the room. Along one side of the table sat her traveling companions thus far. Ortran and Maco sat near the head beside the frowning mayor. Burkus and Paldor took the next two chairs and were flanked on their opposite side by another Ialish gentleman whom Lena recognized from their caravan but had not met. The Ialu in the party were all wearing the laced sleeved tunics she had noticed the night before. The professor paced slowly around the front of the room opposite the mayor as he examined a page from his journal, humming softly to himself.

Seated across the table from Ortran's group was a gentleman of clearly significant social standing who had not yet been introduced. He was a human in his fifties perhaps – well dressed and adorned with bits of gold in all of the appropriate places. Beside him sat a pair of nervous-looking associates, followed by a harried-looking scholarly fellow who was arranging a sheaf of documents on the table. Lena shot a look at Resaka, who leaned on the far wall against a wooden column with his hands in his pockets, looking as disinterested as possible. A pair of crisp town guardsmen stood stiffly at attention along the opposite wall behaving as if they were contestants in a statue impersonation contest. Standing beside the double doors leading to the foyer were two security men in the colors of the wealthy gentleman. From where Lena had taken position between the front doors and the foot of the table, she could see most of the exits to the room and all of its occupants. She stood off to one side, her steel armor clanking softly as she clasped her hands behind her back. A quiet moment ticked by with painful slowness.

The door to the foyer creaked open, and a wizened Ialu in a brown robe hobbled her way into the oak-paneled room, leaning heavily on a gnarled wooden cane. A younger Ialu moved to aid her through the door but was waved off by the older figure. She spared a polite nod to the professor and shuffled into the room, her cane making quiet clacking noises on the glazed brick floor.

"It's about time," the wealthy man spoke indignantly. Mayor Harcort stood and, after glaring at the rich fellow beside him, extended a gesture of greeting across the room.

"Thank you, good madam, for agreeing to meet with us on such short notice." The mayor gestured to a stool at the foot of the table. "Gentleman, allow me to present Rezék Muluvchy, Shaman of the Kopik Tribe." The aged Ialu gave a slight bow, and after a chorus of 'at your service' and 'I yours' from the collected crowd, the shaman sat on the stool and folded her hands in her lap.

"Lovely. Now can we be on with this?" the disgruntled wealthy man at the head of the table beside the mayor asked. "What the devil is this all about?"

"I thank you, Count Xedrin, for your time," Ortran filled in, standing as he spoke. Lena raised an eyebrow. Xedrin? "While it is unfortunate that your cousin the Margrave could not join us here today, I am certain that your esteemed presence, along with the good mayor, represents sufficient authority to conclude the business at hand."

"Which is what exactly?" Xedrin asked.

"I am Vedok Ortran Shalkaat of the Red Hand. It is our purpose to establish that this young man is Maco Skofkaal, rightful heir by direct line of the brothers Uzich and Koldûr Skofkaal. Furthermore, it is our goal to establish his rightful and sole ownership of the iron mines that service the great township of Rafa as provided by the original contract between his esteemed family and Rafa. We are in possession of the necessary documentation to affirm these claims and wish to have the contract certified as such here today." Ortran sat and politely shifted his gaze to the mayor. A moment of stunned silence sat in the room. One of the town guards along the far wall shifted nervously, sacrificing his chance at being proclaimed 'best statue.'

"That is preposterous," Xedrin laughed. "The issue with the contract was settled nearly two hundred years ago. Surely mayor, you won't entertain such nonsense."

"I have examined their preliminary arguments." The mayor trembled slightly as he spoke. "It is possible that there is merit."

"Fine. If we must have another legal battle, then so be it. I will send to Toctil for a magistrate." The count nearly spat the words.

"As fortune would have it, my good Count, we are in the honored company of an Arbiter of the King's Law today." Ortran nearly beamed. "Allow me to introduce Professor Kirstaad Durwynn, teacher of history at the Toctillian Academy of Arts and Sciences and also, as I have mentioned…"

"Him?" Xedrin interrupted. Lena suppressed a smile. It seemed the professor was a sly old fox.

"Indeed." The professor smiled congenially. "At your service."

"I will need to see documentation," Xedrin demanded. The elderly shaman stood and cleared her throat.

"If I may?" she asked to the room. Without waiting for an answer, she gestured for the other Ialu in the room to stand and expose their tattoos. As the men unlaced their sleeves, Rezék closed her eyes and began to utter a soft chant in Ialish. Her voice was dry and quiet, but the sound seemed to fill the room, nonetheless. She made a gesture touching her forehead, then her heart, and in turn, the forehead and heart of each of the Ialu present. The chant seemed to take on a life of its own, swirling around the room, filling the darkened corners with a pulsing rhythm. Lena blinked her eyes as she noticed the tattoo markings on each Ialu began to emit a soft blue glow. The light pulsated across the inked lines, humming with the rhythm of the chant. For a moment, the room was transfixed by the display, and the sound and lights continued as the shaman turned back to her stool at the end of the table. As she fell quiet, the glowing faded, leaving the hall in a state of hushed silence.

"These men are who they say they are. There is no falsehood here." Resék sat, fished a dried apricot from her pocket, and popped it casually in her mouth.

"A shaman has verified Mister Durwynn's credentials as an Arbiter and Mister Skofkaal's family line. The word of a shaman is, of course, without reproach. I propose that we continue with the proceedings," Ortran suggested.

"Absolutely not." Xedrin frowned. "Your arbiter is an Ialu. He's biased."

"Begging your pardon, good sir," the professor spoke. "I do not share Society, Clan, Tribe, or Family with any of the plaintiffs. Therefore, there is no legal basis for me to recuse myself."

"You're Ialish!" Xedrin countered.

"And you fine gentlemen are human," the professor noted. "Should the mayor recuse himself because of his racial affiliation with the aggrieved parties? No? I thought not." He turned to the mayor. "It is my position that these proceedings should continue. I shall preside over them in my official capacity. Do you concur, Mister Mayor?"

"I'm afraid I must," the mayor conceded.

"Nonsense, Latham, surely you won't allow this." Xedrin glowered at the mayor while waving his hand emphatically as if fending off a persistent bee.

"I don't have a choice, Count," the mayor pleaded. "The arbiter is confirmed and has jurisdiction. If I refuse, I could lose my position and possibly face legal repercussions." He gestured imploringly. "My hands are tied."

"Well, I, for one, will not participate in this farce." Xedrin stood and made as if to leave.

"Then I am afraid, Count, that the proceedings will continue without your input, and you would forfeit your right to appeal." The professor walked around behind the humans at the table to stand beside the mayor at the head of the table. "Are there attorneys present?"

"Aye." Paldor stood. "I am Paldor Evinson. I represent Mister Skofkaal."

"Aye." A man beside Xedrin stood as well. "I am Gurik Ludlow. I represent Count Xedrin."

"Ahem." Resék stood. "It seems I am finished here. Many initiates will declare at the festival tonight, and I must prepare my ink and needles." She turned toward the door, leaning on her cane. "Good day to you all," she offered over her shoulder as she left.

"Thank you, kind madam." The professor then turned and nodded to the lawyers. "Gentlemen, do either of you disagree with any of the following statements? First, as legal guardian of this township, the mayor has the authority to accept my jurisdiction and has done so in accordance with the law. Secondly, the identity of Mister Skofkaal has been verified by a shaman of the Ialu people. And lastly, that these proceedings have sufficient legal merit and jurisdiction to continue in this venue."

"I do not disagree," Ludlow muttered.

"Nor I," Paldor followed.

"Indeed," the professor went on. "Then, Mister Ludlow, will you please explain to your client his legal position concerning his participation in these proceedings." The professor smiled. Ludlow adjusted the collar of his jacket, sweating visibly.

"I'm afraid he is right, sir," Ludlow spoke to the count. "If we abandon this process, we forfeit both our say in these matters and our right to appeal." The count had been growing visibly more red-faced with each passing moment, and briefly, Lena feared his head may actually burst.

"Fine. I'll sit through this nonsense," Xedrin agreed and waved his hand as if to allow the show to continue.

"Mister Shalkaat, you have the floor." The professor gestured to Ortran.

"Thank you, sir." Ortran turned to the scholarly human fellow at the far end of the table. "Sir, what is your name?"

"Halad, sir," the man spoke meekly from the end of the table. He stood and shuffled the stack of documents on the table. "Halad Marlan."

"And Mister Marlan, what is your occupation?"

"I'm a scribe, sir. I also maintain the archives here in Rafa and do some work in the mayor's office. The mayor can vouch for me." He gestured toward the harried mayor at the opposite end of the table, who simply nodded in return.

"Do you currently have in your possession, as I have previously requested, the original document that provided for the ownership of the mines in question?"

"Yes, sir, I do." Marlan shuffled through the stack of documents on the table for an inordinate period of time before offering one for inspection.

"All involved parties should review the document," the professor stated. "Mister Ludlow, if you please." The document was read and examined by nearly everyone at the table before the professor went on. "Is there agreement that this document is legitimate?"

"No." Xedrin stood. "As we all understand, documents such as these are signed, verified, and sealed with official Disks of State." He smiled smugly. "Without the original disk, the document cannot be verified, and therefore the claim cannot be considered legitimate." He turned to point at Ortran. "You're finished."

"Mister Shalkaat, can you provide Count Xedrin with the proof he requires?" Durwynn asked.

"I can." Ortran gestured to Burkus.

"Gentlemen." Burkus stood and extended an open hand toward Resaka, who stepped forward carrying a leather satchel. Lena looked at him with a raised eyebrow. Resaka shrugged almost imperceptibly and handed over the satchel.

"I am Burkus Sharath." He opened the satchel and produced an object wrapped in leather. "As you will see, this is the original seal of the Zelshka Kovik used to complete the contract." He unwrapped the disk, placed it on the table, and sat. Xedrin's face went white as he dropped back into his chair.

"Certainly, it is a forgery," he stammered. "The disk was lost."

"There is one way to test it." The professor stepped forward to lift the seal from the table and place it beside the contract. "Mayor?" The mayor let out a pained sigh and produced the seal of the Township of Rafa from a chain around his neck. The professor placed the disks over the stamped sections of the document. They seemed to snap into place as he released them. "Mister Skofkaal, I will need a drop of your blood. Scribe Marlan, please observe." Maco stepped triumphantly around the table, drawing a small knife from his belt as he did so. Marlan begrudgingly approached the head of the table as well. Maco drew the blade across a fingertip and produced a drop of blood which he let fall on the Ialish disk. Both disks let out a low yellowish glow.

"There." Ortran pointed at the document. "Verified."

"Do any of the parties have a legal reason to dispute the veracity of these results?" the professor asked.

"Is there not a requirement for the receiving party to be of the proper clan?" Ludlow asked. "I see Mister Skofkaal has not yet declared for a clan." He pointed to Maco's bare arm where his clan mark would be.

"We have a member of the Zelshka Kovik here with us today. As you can see, he is of a founding family and may speak for his clan," Ortran spoke and gestured to the third Ialu sitting at the end of the table. The fellow rose and displayed his encircled clan marking.

"My name is…" he began.

"I don't care a whit what your name is!" Xedrin interrupted. The Ialu shrugged and sat.

"In any case, the requirement for clan presence is met." Ortran smiled.

"This is a farce!" Xedrin stood angrily. "You think you can just come in here and take my mines?!" He shook visibly.

"You are understandably upset good Count, but may I remind you we are in the midst of a legal proceeding," the professor offered calmly.

"This is not over." The count kicked his chair out from behind him and stormed toward the door.

"Am I to interpret the count's statement as a request for an appeal?" the professor asked. Xedrin paused in the open space by the foot of the table. Ludlow fumbled with his satchel for a moment and managed to stammer a response.

"Yes, uh, yes indeed," he said. "We will appeal." He looked at Xedrin. "Correct, sir?"

"Damn right we will." Xedrin took a menacing step toward the table. Lena noted that he was armed with a ceremonial but still likely functional sword. She adjusted her own sword in its scabbard and shot a glance at the guardsmen.

"Sir?" The third man from the count's side of the table, who until this moment had remained silent, spoke quietly, gesturing to gain the professor's attention.

"Yes?"

"I am Kaldar Murg. I manage the operation of the mine in question."

"Indeed. You may speak."

"I have a contract – an entirely separate document from the ownership papers – that allows me to manage the extraction of the ore from the mine and entitles me to a share of the profits consummate to that responsibility." He stood and gestured to the scribe. Marlan began to shuffle once again through his documents.

"I see," the professor answered. "One thing at a time. Count Xedrin, your request for appeal has been heard. The matter will be referred to the magistrate who is assigned to this district, and a hearing will be scheduled at a later time. Until your

Jason Lancour

appeal is heard, I rule that the ownership of the mine shall revert to the original contract as signed and sealed before us all. Mister Skofkaal is now the legal owner of the iron mines."

"Damn you!" Xedrin bellowed.

"Now, as for Mister Murg…" The professor accepted a document from the scribe and read it closely.

"What are you up to, Murg?" Xedrin rounded on the fellow.

"Business, sir," Murg responded flatly.

"This document is in order," the professor announced.

"Wait, what are you saying?" Ortran asked.

"This contract allows Mister Murg and his company of men the exclusive rights to extract ore from the mines."

"But I own them now!" Maco interjected.

"Quiet boy." Ortran silenced the young man.

"Until such time as the new owners are fit to award a similar contract to another party, this contract possessed by Mister Murg will stand," the professor stated.

"I look forward to working with you sir." Murg smiled at Maco.

"This is outrageous!" Xedrin bellowed. He snapped his head toward the door indicating to his entourage that they should follow and stormed out with a dramatic flip of his expensive cloak.

"Your expertise will be most valuable in the days ahead." Maco smiled smugly. "But don't get too comfortable."

"That's enough, boy." Ortran all but shoved Maco back into his seat. Xedrin's lawyer gathered his documents into his satchel slowly, as if caught in a dream.

"If there is nothing further concerning the issues at hand, I will conclude this proceeding and defer my authority back to the mayor," the professor offered with a slight bow.

"I accept the ruling," Paldor stated.

"I accept, conditionally. Our request for appeal is made," Ludlow mumbled.

"Noted." The professor gestured to the mayor and stepped away from the table.

"I… uh… I declare these proceedings finished. Mister Skofkaal now owns the iron mine," the mayor stammered and sat heavily in his chair, mumbling something about a need for whiskey. Lena wholeheartedly agreed. Ortran, Maco, and Paldor then descended upon the mayor, all but dragging the harried scribe to the head of the table. As they began to hash out some legal details, Lena walked over to the professor.

"You old devil." She smiled at him.

"A title I have earned many times in my years," the professor admitted with a twinkle in his eye. "I trust your recent education found you adequately prepared for this morning's developments?"

"I was able to follow along." She shot a sidelong glance at the guardsmen. One of them had left closely upon Xedrin's heels with a deeply alarmed look on his face. "It feels like this is going to be problematic for a little while yet," she suggested.

"Indeed," the professor admitted. "We are in a lot of danger right now." He looked around the room, making brief eye contact with Burkus, who nodded. "I had hoped to prepare you for this situation as much as possible without violating any trusts."

"I appreciate that, Professor." She watched as Burkus urged the scribe to scribe faster. "What sort of danger are we expecting?"

"Well, the mines have been reclaimed fairly and according to the law." The professor sat on the vacated stool for a moment while the group at the end of the table completed their business. "However, if something unfortunate were to befall Mister Skofkaal before he arrives safely in Nephron, then I'm afraid the mine will revert back to its previous owners."

"And we believe he would be safe in Nephron?" Lena had her doubts. Certainly, being in the home of nearly every Ialu warrior clan lent a certain degree of safety against direct attack. Still, there were many ways to kill a fellow that didn't involve fighting one's way through a thousand or so battle-hardened Ialu soldiers.

"If Maco chooses to sell the contract to another person, or perhaps a legal entity, then he would be out of danger from such things, I suppose."

"Ah." The final piece of the puzzle in Lena's mind just slid into place. "Word is going to spread. Quickly."

"It will."

"A lot of wealthy people are going to be very displeased with this turn of events."

"I'd imagine so."

"So, we need to get the hell out of town," Lena finished.

"I couldn't agree more."

"I'm already packed," she acknowledged, striding across the room to peer through the window. She hadn't known precisely what the professor and Ortran had planned, but her instincts had suggested that she be ready to leave quickly. She felt doubly glad she had decided to don her full armor today. Gazing through the window, she saw the morning's festival crowd had already begun to amass, and she saw several townsfolk strolling around, with ale already in hand. The town hall was positioned on a slight rise, one block away from the open square that faced the Stoneheart Inn. Lena spied one of the count's goons across the cobblestone street, leaning on a lamp post.

"I think we are in some deep shit," Resaka offered from behind her as he approached her position by the window.

"Isn't that the truth. Those boys need to get their paperwork done quickly." She glanced at the group around the table. Men were standing, shaking hands, and clapping each other on the shoulders, but no one seemed inclined to vacate the building just yet. She let out an exasperated breath. "Are you ready to ride?" she asked Resaka.

"Yeah. After your flash of intuition last night, it seemed wise to be prepared to leave quickly."

"Well, let's see what these boys have in mind for us." Lena spied Burkus as he began to herd the group toward the front door. The mayor had removed himself through a door in the rear of the room, no doubt in search of a stiff drink.

"We are going to return to the inn as calmly as possible." Ortran addressed the group quietly as they all huddled together. "I won't dictate to anyone else what they should do, but Maco, Burkus, and I are going to collect our things and leave for Nephron with my company of soldiers immediately. Anyone who wishes to come along is welcome." He looked squarely at the professor as she finished.

"I feel like my work in Rafa is finished." The professor nodded. "I would join you on the road."

"It would be a pleasure, sir." Ortran gave a slight bow.

"If I may?" Lena interjected. Ortran nodded. "Xedrin's men are watching the doors. None of us knows what they've got planned, but I'd be stunned if they simply let us go about our merry way."

"I wouldn't expect an attack inside the walls," Burkus added. "Too many of your fellow Red Hand soldiers here. Even not knowing what the trouble was about, they would certainly jump to our defense."

"Agreed," Ortran said. "I think Miss Sullivan makes a valid point, however. We would be fools not to expect trouble once we are away from the walls."

"Are any of your units accompanied by a mage?" Lena asked Ortran.

"Unfortunately, not. The Mage's Guild forbids formal enrollment of its members within military units, except for medical and non-combat related functions."

"I wonder if it would be worth our while to stop by our caravan encampment on the way out," Resaka suggested. "It's possible that Zahra would allow us to employ Pevma's services for a time. Informally, of course."

"I'm afraid that, as a representative of the Servé Ruche, if I am paying her, it would still be illegal." Ortran shook his head.

"Assuming both Pevma and Zahra are willing, I could hire Pevma to accompany me," Burkus offered. "As personal security."

"I suppose that is a different matter." Ortran nodded. "Worth investigating, I suppose."

"How much time will we need before we can ride?" Lena asked. "I am ready to go immediately." She tapped her steel shoulder guard.

"Five minutes at the most," Resaka added, glancing at Burkus for confirmation.

"My men are already assembled," Ortran stated. "If there is nothing further, then we should be off." He turned and pushed through the heavy oak doors into the foyer and out into the cobblestone street.

CHAPTER EIGHT

Lena handed the field glass back to Vochny. She could make out the force that had been trailing them for the last day and a half with her naked eye now, but the magnification of the glass helped significantly. Vochny raised the brass cylinder to his eye and surveyed the opposing force.

"What do you see?" Pevma asked. They were crouched along a ridge overlooking the road trailing behind them back toward Rafa. Lena had been surprised that Pevma had agreed to join them, though not as surprised as Ortran had been. Even though Burkus had made an offer of significant generosity, it seemed the Ialish captain did not expect a person of Selyrian heritage to come to the aid of his own people. They were barely underway for a day before everyone was glad that she had. The night before last, her magic had detected a group of Goblins in the near vicinity – a group that had steadily grown in size over the past day. If the Goblins had remained undetected, it was likely that their own position would have been far more desperate already.

"It's like we thought." Lena felt an urge to keep her voice down, even though the enemy was still in the distance. "No way to tell precise numbers, but I'd guess they've got us by at least four to one."

"I see him," Vochny stated, offering the glass to Pevma. "Xedrin's man." He pointed across the valley to the low ridge across from them. "Tall fellow. Only one on a horse."

"Ah." Pevma peered through the glass. "Agreed."

"Four to one may be optimistic." Vochny turned away from the valley below. "Experience has taught me to expect two more Goblins for each one you can see."

"Ten or twelve to one then, worst case." Lena ground her teeth. The animosity between the local Goblin population and the Red Hand Ialu had been made clear already, but the speed with which Xedrin's men had been able to gather the force facing them was still impressive. "Twenty-seven of us, a few hundred of them. What's to worry about?" Lena supposed that the Goblin's intense distaste for Ialu was sufficient for them to set aside their feelings concerning the men of Rafa.

"We are mounted. They are on foot," Pevma noted, handing the field-glass back to Vochny. "We should be able to outrun them."

"If this were flat, open ground, I would agree." Vochny collapsed the brass tube on itself and tucked it into his belt. "In this rough terrain, though, the road curves back on itself too often." He shook his head. "Goblins can cut through the forest far more easily than we can. They'll catch us before nightfall."

"Do you know this road well?" Lena asked. Vochny nodded. "Is there an open place we can assemble to mount a charge? We have the advantage of horse."

"Nothing large enough." Vochny half stood and retreated from the ridge at a crouch. "Besides, the velni horse is not ideal for cavalry."

"Why Goblins?" Pevma asked coolly. "Certainly, the count has enough professional soldiers to do the job."

"He wouldn't dare openly attack the Red Hand with his own troops," Vochny answered. "That would be like a declaration of war. Our people would retaliate."

"I'm surprised at the restraint," Pevma commented as they walked back toward the path. "Rich men seem to have a talent for starting things they can't finish."

"I cannot disagree with you, miss." Vochny shook his head. "As for a finish, however, these Goblins seem sufficient to the task, unfortunately."

"We should report back." Lena and Pevma silently followed the soldier back toward their group, each lost in their own thoughts. Nothing about their situation was preferable, and she wondered not for the first time since leaving home if this day might be her last. Given the Goblin penchant for ambush and harassment tactics, if she and her company kept on their current course, they would undoubtedly be dead to the last long before reaching Nephron and never once face their enemy in open combat. Ortran took the news grimly but held his resolve. After a brief discussion in Ialish with his lieutenant and the professor, he turned to address the group as a whole.

"Our memory of this area suggests that there is a narrow point on the road ahead. I'm sending scouts forward to assess its defensive potential." Ortran gestured to the path behind him as two lightly armored Ialu bolted past on their stubby horses. "A fight is coming whether we seek it or not. I intend to fight this battle on our own terms. Prepare yourselves." He dismissed his group with a wave, and the men fell about the task of readying themselves to ride. Lena spied the professor amongst the group. He bore a wide-bladed short sword around his waist.

"Perhaps we should have stayed in Rafa after all," the professor said with a sad chuckle. "I'm sorry to have dragged you into this mess."

"We're not dead yet," Lena answered. "Though, I think we might be if we had stayed in Rafa. A man like Xedrin isn't going to hang his hopes on the rematch of a legal battle he has already lost."

"Indeed." The professor nodded. "Without wanting to sound boastful, my legal rendering of the subject was solid as stone. A magistrate will find no different result, and I believe his lawyer knows that."

"Xedrin is no fool. He is going to use different tactics for this next round. For him to get what he wants, we would need to be removed from the equation completely. A convenient accident. Fall from a window, perhaps. Or poison." Lena offered her hand to aid the professor into his saddle. "I don't envy Paldor. Staying behind was risky."

"Xedrin gains nothing by moving against him. The legal battle is done," the professor stated. "And Maco needed Paldor there to address the legal particulars of the mine's profits until such time as our young friend is in a position to address the finances himself."

"I still think I'd rather be out here, where I know who my enemies are."

"Nonetheless." The professor allowed her assistance as he heaved himself into the saddle. "This is hardly the job you agreed to. I myself didn't know the full extent of the hornet's nest I was sticking my unwanted nose into."

"What do you mean?" Lena asked.

"At first, I truly *was* writing a book on the history of the Red Hand." The professor leaned forward slightly and lowered his voice. The Ialu soldiers paid them no heed, but the professor shot a conspiratorial look over his shoulder, nonetheless. "My research on the subject brought my attention to the tribal records of the Skofkaal family. A fair bit of persistence and digging led me to young Maco over there. But when I arrived at his home to conduct an interview, I discovered that Ortran and his fellows had already whisked him away toward Rafa. The rest of my involvement has resulted from my own foolish curiosity."

"I see." Anyone could see that the hearing in Rafa had been meticulously planned well in advance. She wondered how deeply involved the professor had been in the process.

"I joined their caravan north under the guise of a traveling historian – which was mostly true incidentally. Ortran began to be suspicious that my interest in his business was more than simple curiosity. After the first time he had me attacked, I thought it prudent to hire some protection." He tilted his head meekly. "Luckily, I was able to gain his confidence as of late, and together we were able to aid our young friend Maco."

"The *first* time?" Lena asked. "Are you suggesting that the guy who jumped us in the alley was Ortran's doing?"

"I suspect so."

"And you're okay with that?" Lena felt her blood begin to rise.

"I suppose I am." He shrugged. "The man wanted to protect his delicate enterprise. It was a strategically prudent maneuver."

"Well, I'm *not* okay with it." Lena squared her shoulders. If they all survived the day, she would have words with Ortran.

"I suppose we have a more pressing issue at hand," Durwynn said solemnly.

"I suppose we do," she admitted and turned to climb into her saddle. One fight at a time.

* * * * *

Ortran's scouts had indeed found a nearly perfect point to turn and face their foes. The last few furlongs of road had been carved out of the mountain along the edge of a steep, rocky incline. To one side was a nearly sheer rock wall, and to the other, a very rapid drop to a ravine below. Ortran had stopped the company just around a slight bend after the road had double backed on itself. From where Lena stood on the road with Resaka and three Ialish archers, the path they had taken to arrive here trailed away to their right in nearly a straight line for several hundred paces. It sloped slightly downward before it doubled back to cross directly in front of their line of sight across a gap of just over a hundred paces. If the enemy moved as expected, the Goblins would have to charge along the road with their flank exposed to archery fire for three hundred paces or so before turning to charge the last two hundred paces uphill toward their position. The shot across the narrow ravine was at the long end of what Lena felt was effective for choosing a specific target, but firing in volleys would still have a noticeable effect. In a perfect scenario, they would have more archers and launch masses of arrows into the area as the Goblins charged through, but then again, if this were a perfect scenario, there wouldn't be any Goblins chasing them at all.

The rest of the company was arrayed just out of sight around the next bend in the road. A phalanx of five heavily armored Ialu standing shoulder to shoulder would create a barricade of steel blocking the entire width of the road. The stone towered up on one side, forming an effective wall for their right flank, and on their left, the topography dropped rapidly into the ravine, making it impossible for the Goblins to encircle them. By placing themselves behind the natural curve to the land, the company of Ialu was safe from return archery fire, and the Goblins would only be able to face them in (relatively) small numbers at any one time.

The plan was for Lena and her archer companions to assail the Goblins as much as possible as they approached and then turn to run once the enemy had moved in close. The hope was to draw the bulk of the Goblin force into pursuit, thinking the archers to be a straggling rearguard of a still moving force. If they could lure the Goblins into charging, she and her companions might be able to wreak a fair toll before the Goblins either fell back or found a way around by climbing one side or the other of the mountain.

If the Goblins played along, the strategy was as sound as it could be. Though physically, Goblins varied significantly in size, the average Goblin was not much larger than a child of a dozen years. Even though their wiry bodies held a surprising strength for their size, individually, they were no match for Ialu soldiers. It was unlikely any of them bore armor beyond whatever leather they could hunt, and their weaponry would likewise be of poor quality. Lena was unaware of any training programs that Goblins would employ to impart to their ranks any appreciable skill in arms – all facts that favored her party. On the other side, the Ialish soldiers were each a fortress of steel by comparison. The

Red Hand footmen were each equipped with heavy plate armor, thick shields, and hardened steel weaponry. The physical strength and combat skill of the Ialish warrior clans were legendary. A shield wall five men wide and three deep should be nearly impenetrable to the Goblin horde.

Victory was far from a foregone conclusion, however. Aside from outnumbering the Ialish company by a very significant margin, the Goblins also had the advantage of pure animal ferocity. What a fighter lacked in skill or power could often be replaced with brutal savagery. She had heard first-hand accounts of Goblin fighters throwing themselves onto their enemies' weapons simply to bear them down so their companions could strike freely. Once the battle was engaged, it was going to get ugly very quickly. Another advantage in the Goblin's favor was their almost preternatural ability to outmaneuver their opponents. To expect the Goblins to smash themselves to pieces against the Ialish shield wall until their entire strength was spent went beyond simple optimism and ventured into near foolishness. Nevertheless, this plan was all they had at the moment. Lena plucked lightly on her bowstring, squinting against the glare of the greying sky as she peered into the shadows of the trees where the first sign of Goblin scouts would appear.

Resaka had borrowed a bow from one of the Ialish soldiers. Given that both he and Lena lacked shields and the cohesive unit training of the Ialu warriors, they would be more of a hindrance than of any help with the shield wall. Resaka had talked his way into being with the archery group and tested the newly acquired bow as best as he could without wasting their precious few arrows. The bow itself was a bit shorter than his stated preference, but it was stout – having nearly the same draw weight as Lena's longbow.

She glanced up at the sky. Heavy grey clouds were gathering just past the far ridge, and though it was still mid-day, the imminent threat of rain began to make the forested mountain feel more like twilight. Best to remain vigilant.

"Anybody care to make a wager?" Resaka asked playfully.

"What do you have in mind?" an Ialish soldier named Hagen asked.

"I'd be willing to bet we take out at least half of them before we all die," Resaka offered with a chuckle.

"What are the stakes?" Hagen asked.

"Does it matter?"

"Quiet," Lena hissed. She shook her head, doing her best to appear annoyed. No need to encourage the boys. Just then, in the deepening shadows across the ravine, she thought she saw movement. "Look there." She gestured for the men to be still. They crouched down behind the thick underbrush bordering the road. "Movement."

"I see them." Urzbek, the ranking Ialu in their advance group, gestured for his men to be ready. "Hold the volley till my mark," he whispered. Lena watched as a pair of Goblin scouts emerged warily onto the trail beyond. It was improbable she and her companions could be seen from their hiding place as long as they remained quiet and motionless. Lena and her companions had applied what the Ialu called *schkova* to their metal armor. Mixing the chalky brown powder with water created a light, fast-drying paste that, when applied to a metallic surface, dulled its reflective qualities almost completely. She had seen mud used for the same purpose, but *schkova* was preferable by far. She and her allies were all but invisible behind the shrubs that concealed them. If she lived to see Nephron, Lena planned to acquire some for future use.

Urzbek held their fire as more Goblins began to emerge along the trail. As much as her professional experience was varied, this would be her first encounter with the legendary foe. From this distance, their forms did indeed resemble adolescent humans, but the size and shape were where the comparison ended. Their posture was decidedly more feral; some walked with their hips open, hunching forward to touch the ground with a hand every half dozen steps. Several stooped to sniff the ground as they moved along the trail. They all loped forward with an air of hunting coyotes, stopping to peer around cautiously as they tracked Lena and her companions.

"Hold," Urzbek whispered. More Goblins began to take the trail, walking with a visibly lower degree of caution than their brethren. The first few had yet to gain the switchback that would put them in line with her position. Urzbek waited for a beat longer. If the forward-most pair of Goblins spotted them first, then much of their advantage would be lost as their targets sprang into more frenetic motion. "On my mark, we target the largest group straight ahead," Urzbek whispered as he fitted an arrow to his string. Lena felt the feathered end of her own missile fit snugly onto her bowstring. She mentally rehearsed standing, drawing, and releasing. "Not yet," Urzbek cautioned. Lena risked a glance away from her target group to the bend in the road to her right. The Goblins had nearly gained the turn. "Now," he whispered the order.

As a group, they all stood and silently released their first volley. Lena watched her arrow fly for just a moment to gauge any necessary adjustments to her aim. The flight of arrows whispered into the midst of the largest group of Goblins, felling two immediately.

"Again. Same group," Urzbek ordered calmly. The Goblins paused in confusion for only a moment. A moment was all that was needed for the second volley to fall in beside the first. Several more Goblins fell, though Lena could not tell if they were hit or simply dropping for cover. "Group to the left. Hold. And, fire." Their third volley ripped into the thinner group just behind their initial targets. Another fell. Those Goblins who had turned to run from the arrows balked, fearing to run into another barrage. "First group. Ready. Fire." Urzbek ordered a volley into the now confused and hesitant mass of Goblin raiders that were not yet running for cover. Two more fell.

"Incoming to our right," Lena warned. A group of Goblins who were cut off from the main body had split. Half were running back along the path to safety behind the bend in the road, daring to run the gauntlet of archery fire. The other half, around five individuals, had decided to try their luck at rushing their position.

"Resaka. Hagen. Take them. Fire at will," Urzbek ordered, not turning his attention away from the trail across the ravine. "Lena, Klavny. Fire on the lead group of runners." His calm was impressive. "Ready. Fire." Lena loosed at the fastest runner from Goblins, who had been cut off from their main group as they ran along the road. Her shot streaked across the abyss and caught the fellow low in the side as he ran.

"Fine shot," the Ialu to her right, Klavny, commented.

"One more. Loose at will," Urzbek ordered. Lena lined up a shot but held back as the last Goblins on the trail either fell or vanished. She had a feeling they would run out of arrows long before they ran out of foes. No sense in wasting shafts. She turned to her right; her arrow still knocked. Only two of the approaching Goblins remained. Resaka and Hagen were both fitting arrows to string when she loosed hers, catching the faster of the two Goblins full in the chest. Seeing he was running into certain death, the last Goblin turned and threw himself over the steep incline to his right, tumbling out of sight into the thicket below.

"Anybody see him?" Hagen asked, half drawing an arrow as he stepped toward the edge. Lena heard crashing in the foliage below, but it was impossible to discern if any of the sounds were made deliberately.

"He won't try anything on his own," Urzbek stated. "Hold position." They waited in silence for a moment, surveying the road across the ravine. Lena could see movement from a few injured Goblins as they struggled to remove themselves from the ambush site.

"Should we retrieve any arrows?" Hagen asked, gesturing to the fallen Goblins to their right.

"No," Urzbek ordered. "They are watching us. If they think we are low on arrows, they will be emboldened."

"Nice work, boys," Resaka congratulated his fellows. "...and lady," he added quickly.

"The next wave won't be nearly so easy," Urzbek stated. "Stay sharp."

It was not long before Urzbek was proven correct. The next wave burst from around the corner without warning. They rushed in at a full sprint, filling the width of the entire road. Row after row of Goblins surged from out of the shadows as a long deep blast of a hunting horn echoed off the mountainside.

"Well shit," Resaka muttered. "There goes my bet."

"Target the front," Urzbek ordered as they stood to draw. "Loose." Their arrows tore into the incoming horde, dropping a few but the stream of Goblinkind continued unabated. "Same," came the order. "Fire." Another volley ripped into the front runners. "One more at the front." The arrows had felled a handful of the enemy, but with the wave of snarling Goblins rolling toward them, their arrows had no more effect than rocks thrown at a tidal wave.

"That's a lot of Goblins," Klavny stated calmly.

"Target straight across. Fire at will," Urzbek ordered. Lena turned away from the front runners who had, at this point, exceeded effective range. She loosed two shafts into the seething mass of enemies, unsure if her arrows were having any effect. She could see where fallen Goblins obstructed the path for their fellows only by where the running Goblins consistently leapt over the same place in the road. The stream of Goblins coming around the corner still hadn't stopped. "Turn right. Form up!" Urzbek barked. The archer group pivoted to align themselves across the width of the road, turning to face the onrushing Goblins head-on. "Draw and hold." Lena pulled an arrow to her cheek. "Loose."

The volley of arrows sliced into the front line of Goblins, dropping four. Lena fitted another arrow to the string and pulled it to her cheek. Urzbek was making the most out of their volleys, waiting until all archers were ready before shooting. They loosed two more volleys, felling their foes with nearly every shot. Urzbek held the line for another moment. In the darkening light beneath the rain clouds, it was difficult to make out individual Goblins. The approaching horde looked as if it were a homogenous seething mass of limbs, weapons, and furious faces. The effect was terrifying.

"Now, break!" He turned and ran back along the road. Lena wasted no time turning on her heel and bolting back around the corner. As she and the others pounded past the rocky outcropping of the ravine wall, she saw the Ialish line had already parted neatly down the middle to allow them through. Urzbek was the last one through as the shield wall closed in behind him.

"Archers!" Ortran shouted. "Watch our left flank!" He was seated on his horse behind the line where he could see the entire engagement area. The weak point of their position was their left side, facing the open ravine. The Goblins would try to exploit that by dribbling soldiers a few paces down along the steep ground and attempting to climb back up the hill toward the entrenched Ialu. The incline was not quite vertical, but any Goblin unlucky enough to find himself fighting up that hill toward an armored position would be at a significant disadvantage. Lena stopped directly behind the last footman in the line, settling herself into a useable firing position. The others lined up behind her, waiting. The closest Ialish soldier turned to her.

"Did you save any for us?" he asked with a gleam in his eye.

"You might get a chance at one or two," she answered with a forced smile, striving to believe in her own bravado.

"Very kind of you." He turned back toward the sloping edge – spear held ready. A beat later, the Goblins rushed around the corner, howling like maniacs. Without a moment's hesitation, they smashed into the Ialu line, and the chaos began in earnest. Even though Lena stood a head taller than the Ialu soldiers, a slight downward slope made it difficult for her to see past the stout backs of the soldiers directly in front of her. The shrieks of dying Goblins and the clatter of weapons clanging on the Ialish shields drowned out the sound of the rain as it began to fall. She snapped her attention to the hillside as a few Goblin fighters tumbled over the edge, seemingly forced aside by the ferocity of their brethren.

The hapless figures careened down the hill and out of sight into the bracken. Lena saved her arrows. Only moments after the initial engagement, the Ialu soldier on the left corner of the front line was borne bodily over the edge as Goblins flung themselves atop his shield, heedless of his sword slashes. He disappeared almost immediately into the underbrush below with three Goblins still clinging to his armor. Another soldier lunged forward to take his place, the rear strap of his armor held fast by his companion behind him. The spearmen directly behind the front line shifted their emphasis to protect the newly revealed weak point in their defense.

Lena ground her teeth in frustration. This type of mass combat was not to her liking. Better to face foes in the open with room to brandish a sword than to be crushed in together like fish in a barrel of steel and blood.

Another Goblin fell off the side but arrested his descent by flailing his arms out wide. He slid a few paces down the hill before catching himself on a sapling. He slowly turned and struggled back up the hill toward the Ialish line. Lena's arrow caught him between the collarbone and the neck, dropping him immediately.

"Aww. I thought you said you'd save me some," the Ialu in front of her joked.

"You gotta be faster," she retorted. She risked a glance over her shoulder. Ortran had decided to keep Pevma in reserve, both as an element of surprise and to conserve her strength if the company got into a jam. She sat on horseback just behind the Ialish commander. Ortran was armed with a bow and occasionally loosed a shaft over the heads of his fellows into the Goblin masses as he shouted orders to his men. Burkus, Maco, and the professor were all also mounted. It was decided that if things got too ugly, they would turn to run and try their best to outpace the Goblins while the soldiers held off the pursuit as long as possible. All three had swords drawn and watched the battle with palpable tension. Behind them all, the rest of the horses paced nervously in place along the road. They had been staked down, but if any of them panicked, they would all likely tear free and bolt down the road. Lena was impressed by the horses' discipline.

The rain began to fall more steadily, drops plinking off of her armor as she turned back to the ravine. She plucked her bowstring again to prevent it from accumulating water, grinding her teeth with a feeling of uselessness. All of the fighting was confined to the single row of armored Ialu in the front. Each bore a tall, rectangular shield that overlapped with the fellow beside him and effectively formed a wall of steel. The shield men in the front held a short sword for stabbing or slashing in their other hand but would only attack if a Goblin made too much progress attempting to wiggle through their ranks. Thus, most of the actual killing was accomplished by the spearmen directly behind the front line. These soldiers held their long-bladed spears overhead and thrust forward past their compatriots' shoulders into the Goblin horde.

The spearmen were taking quite a toll on their enemies as they stabbed over and over into the seething mass of fury. A third row of spearmen stood by with spears held ready but did not engage unless there was a clear and distinct opening for attack. The shrieks of pain and clatter of Goblin weapons against the iron shields was noise enough to nearly wake the dead and rattled Lena's nerves far more than it would if she was able to take part in the battle. Something about standing still while a ferocious battle raged on three paces away was far more unnerving than Lena would have imagined. Occasionally another Goblin would tumble into her line of sight, but none could hold the steep ground for more than an instant.

The Goblins threw themselves at the Ialish line with the ferocity of demons. Lena saw one Goblin climb on the backs of his dying kin to hurl himself bodily over the line. An Ialish spear skewered him neatly through the middle, but he simply grabbed the spear with both hands and pulled it through his body as a means to clawing his way closer to his foes. The fellows supporting him collapsed as one was cut down, and the impaled Goblin fell out of sight to the mud below, wrenching the spear from the grasp of the Ialu soldier. The spear was immediately replaced by a soldier behind him, and the carnage continued.

A Goblin body came soaring through the air, seemingly launched by his fellows, and crashed atop a soldier in the front line, bearing him to the ground as another Goblin grabbed hold of his shield. He disappeared from view, but the clatter of weapons on metal grew louder and more ferocious as he was dragged off onto the swirling maelstrom of Goblin bodies. The line adjusted quickly as the man behind him stepped forward, slinging his shield to bear from his back and locking in place with his fellows in the front. Spears thrust forward, churning like some great machine in a storybook sorcerer's tower, producing screams and blood with each cycle. How long the battle raged on was difficult to tell, as Lena stood silent, helpless, and ready at her position on their flank.

The assault ended as abruptly as it began with the final thunk of an Ialish blade connecting with Goblin bone. Without an audible command, the Goblins assailing their position suddenly turned and ran back down the road, rapidly disappearing around the rocky bend. Within moments the Ialu stood alone, the road in front of them littered with fallen Goblins. They had lost four of their own.

"Should we pursue, sir?" an Ialish voice rang out.

"No," Ortran replied. "Could be a trap. Line advance five paces and hold. Wounded fall back. Second row, retrieve our dead. Watch for pretenders." The front line of five marched forward steadily, making certain as they went that any Goblins who were currently on the ground would remain there permanently. The crunch of metal against bone made an unsettling sound as the soldiers methodically cleared the field of survivors. The three Ialu who had fallen in the front were pulled back to the rear, along with three others who were seriously wounded. Of the fourth of their losses, the soldier who had been pulled into the ravine, there was no sign. Pevma dismounted and began to attend to the wounded.

"Dulza?" an Ialish soldier shouted toward the downslope. No response. "Sir?" The soldier turned to look at Ortran. The commander raised a hand to request silence. He repeated.

"Dulza!" They all strained to hear sounds from their fallen comrade. The only sound was the rain steadily rattling the foliage of the forest around them. "I need eyes around that corner," Ortran stated, gesturing to the bend in the road where the Goblins had retreated.

"I'll go," Lena spoke up. The Ialu soldier guarding the slope beside her hissed softly. "Still too slow," she chided him in a whisper.

"Proceed." Ortran gestured to the front line. "Hagen. You too." The line parted down the center as she and Hagen stepped forward. She shouldered her bow and drew her sword.

"Have that bow ready," she urged Hagen as she eased around the corner. Keeping herself at a distance from the rock wall in case any Goblins were feeling simultaneously vicious and suicidal, Lena stepped out into the path to gain a view down the road back toward Rafa.

No living Goblins were in sight for the length of the slope down toward the switchback. She scanned the road and surrounding shrubs. There was nowhere to hide any substantial force. The Goblins they had shot during the initial rush were still sprawled where they had fallen. It was possible that during the retreat, some had lowered themselves over the side of the slope to remain close, but to get back upright and onto the road's surface would take some struggle. There was no way to leap out quickly.

She glanced across the ravine. A few stragglers milled around in the shadows on the path across the gap, but the rain obscured their numbers. "Keep eyes on the road," she urged Hagen quietly. Turning to Ortran, she gave a commonly used all-clear signal. Responding with only a nod, Ortran gave a hand signal, and two Ialu with long hooks began to clear the road of the fallen Goblins. They dragged the fallen toward the edge of the ravine, dumping them unceremoniously over the side. Any Goblins who attempted to approach from below would need to stumble through a heap of their deceased fellows.

"Sir, what about Dulza?" one of the Ialu soldiers asked. Ortran scowled. No commander wanted to abandon a fallen comrade, but the risk of sending a team down to confirm what in all likelihood was his death was an enormous hazard to the rest of the company.

"I can get down there," Resaka offered, gesturing down the slope. "They'll never see me." He winked and hefted the collar of his black cloak.

"Do it. Be quick." Ortran grimaced. Resaka handed his bow to the professor and adjusted the fit of his thick, hardened leather armor. Without a sound, he slipped down the edge of the slope and vanished. Be careful, you idiot, she silently warned him. Lena re-sheathed her sword and shifted the bow back into her left hand, knocking an arrow. She and Hagen kept their eyes on the road as the Ialu finished the grisly work of clearing the field of the dead. She occasionally tapped her bow against her metal shin guard to knock the rain droplets from the string and arrow. In this weather, she wouldn't have much effective range at all – maybe one shot at a charging group before having to turn to run for the shield wall.

The rain splattered in fat droplets on her and her fellows, making rivulets of mud across the road's surface. If this kept up, the footing would become treacherous. She could see indistinct movement on the trail across the gap, but it was scattered and random. While it was difficult to make out any individual foes, another massed charge like the first would still be clearly noticeable.

"I'm afraid," Hagen admitted in a whisper. He was young. Not much older than Maco. If he had seen battle before, it could not have been often. Droplets of rain trickled off the rim of his helmet and ran over his clenched jaw, disappearing into the collar of the gambeson he wore beneath his steel armor.

"Good," Lena responded quietly. "You'd be a damn fool if you weren't." Hagen nodded halfheartedly. "Just leave that part out when you are telling the ladies back home," she added with a smirk. He smiled faintly in response. Lena shot a glance over her shoulder and saw Resaka climbing back over the edge of the drop. He was alone. He exchanged a quiet word with Ortran, shaking his head.

"Hey, what's that?" Hagen pointed across the ravine. Lena squinted into the grey. It looked to be a figure on horseback slowly making his way along the road.

"Don't know. Nothing good, I imagine." She turned to Ortran and waved. "I think we've got something," she said. "Mounted figure."

"One?" he asked.

"Looks that way," she answered. "You want me to shoot him?"

"Not yet." Ortran sat on his mount thoughtfully. "Let's see what he wants. If he looks like a mage, stop him before he gets close."

"Aye," Hagen responded, readying his bow. Lena watched the horse walk with painful slowness down the path and around the corner. As the figure began to approach, Lena was able to discern that it was the fellow they had earlier supposed to be Xedrin's man. A tall Goblin marched beside the horse, arming himself with iron weapons and armor. While he still stood no taller than any of the Ialu, he was thicker than most of his Goblin brethren and carried himself with more confidence. Lena supposed he was some sort of unit commander for the Goblins if there was such a thing.

Just as the horseman began to near what Lena estimated was the maximum effective range for shooting in the rain, he pulled his mount to a stop. He sat quietly in his saddle, looking at Lena and Hagen with an entirely disinterested air. Finally, after a moment of silence, Lena spoke.

"Yes?" She had to raise her voice to a near shout to project the distance over the soaking rain.

"Your commander, if you please," he shouted back. With a shrug, Lena turned to Ortran. He swung a leg over his mount, dropped to the muddy road, and made his way through the shield line, striding around the corner with a distinctly irritated air.

"I command this unit," Ortran shouted, folding his steel-covered arms over his breastplate. "Step forward. I don't feel like shouting." The man dismounted as well and approached slowly with the Goblin at his side. The pair stopped a few paces off. "Well?"

"We just want the boy," he said plainly.

"If that's all you have to say, then you're wasting our time," Ortran responded disgustedly.

"You have fought well, but we both know you won't leave this place alive," the man spoke again. "Give us the boy, and we promise no harm will befall him." He placed his hands over his heart. "You may leave here peacefully, or you can all die in the mud. Your choice," he finished with a matter-of-fact tone, placing a hand on the hilt of the tapered longsword hanging on his hip. Ortran stroked his jaw absently and began to pace. Not wanting to spoil the moment with a slip of a wet bowstring, Lena lowered her aim, relaxing her bow slightly.

"You say no harm will befall the young man?" he asked, stepping closer. "Why would you spare him?"

"My partners would like to make him a business offer. He can't sign any papers if he is dead."

"True, true." Ortran nodded and paced around the road. "I suppose you'll offer him a fair price," he stated.

"Of course, you have my..." The man's response was cut short as Ortran drew his sword and sliced his leg off in one single motion. Ortran arced his blade in a tight circle and swept the man's head clean from his shoulders before he hit the ground. The Goblin drew his own blade and pointed it at Ortran, his eyes wide. Lena's sword was in her hand before she realized she had drawn it. Her bow rattled on the ground beside her. Hagen stood next to her; an arrow pulled to his cheek.

For a moment, there was stillness. Rain splattered in the mud and the blood while the dead man's body gave one final twitch. Ortran's eyes were fire, and Lena could see the water droplets flying from his lips as he panted in anger through clenched teeth. He slammed his sword back into its scabbard and took a menacing step forward as if he intended to rend the Goblin apart with his gauntleted fists. The Goblin took an unconscious step back, nearly stumbling on a loose stone. Ortran bent down, lifted the deceased man's head with both hands, and drove forward, impaling the grisly trophy on the point of the Goblin's blade.

"There's my answer," he growled. "Run back to your masters and have another go at us. I hope you brought enough of your brothers to feed our steel." The Goblin grabbed his weapon with both hands, struggling to keep it raised with the added weight of a human head.

"Our king will bathe in your blood," he said in a gravelly voice that was strangely deep for someone of his size. "We will..."

"Enough!" Brushing the Goblin's weapon aside with one hand, Ortran took a step forward and jabbed a steel-encased finger against the Goblin's chest. "Turn away now. Or none of you will see the sunrise," Ortran finished in an even tone, staring into the Goblin's face, almost daring him to try something. The two glared at each other for a moment longer. Lena shot a cautious look over the edge of the path in case this whole display had been merely a diversion. She saw nothing but the grey rain falling amongst the leaves below.

The Goblin backed away slowly, pointing his still burdened sword at their group. After several paces, he turned and walked back toward his brethren with as much dignity as he could muster. The man's horse turned on its own and followed the Goblin back down the road. Soon the all traces of their enemy were lost behind the veil of rain.

"I don't think their king is going to like your message," Lena suggested coolly.

"Ha!" Ortran chuckled. "If he doesn't like that one, he is definitely not going to like what I have to say when I see him face to face." Ortran turned and walked back toward his company. "Hagen. Urzbek. Keep eyes on that road."

"Aye," Urzbek responded and stepped forward from the formation, bow held ready.

"Vochny. Status." The line parted smoothly for Ortran as he spoke, striding confidently back to his vantage point. Lena followed and resumed her place on the edge of the road.

"Including our archery barrages, I estimate we have accounted for fifty, maybe sixty of their number," Vochny stated. "We lost Aelgar, Berin, and Kelix." He followed in a softer tone.

"Mister Devash has told me that Dulza is also lost," Ortran spoke through clenched teeth. "Damn you, Xedrin," he muttered. "Miss Pevma, what of the wounded?"

"Two are back on their feet and declare themselves fit for duty. Given our strategic position, I must reluctantly agree." She stood from where she had been crouching next to the third wounded soldier. "However, this stubborn fellow cannot stand…"

"I can stand!" the soldier protested. He shifted his weight as if he intended to prove his assertation, but Pevma held him down.

"I do not believe he is fit for combat," she finished.

"Can he sit on a horse?" Ortran asked.

"For a little while," she answered.

"A little while may be all we have." Ortran turned away. "Klavny, bring him a mount and give him a bow. You'll take his position on the line." Ortran turned to face the group as a whole. "They are going to throw everything they have at us next time. Let's protect our left corner. I want a man in the second row with both hands on the corner guard. Keep low and let the spearman to your right defend you. The rest of the second row shift your attention appropriately. That's four spears doing the job of five. I won't lose another man down the hill. Understood?"

"Aye!" the men shouted back. As Ortran called a few more orders to organize his men, Lena stepped closer to Resaka.

"How does it look down there?" she asked, throwing a look over the side of the road into the ravine.

"There's a flat spot about thirty paces down," he responded. "It tapers off back down into the ravine. It won't be an easy trip to get there from the other side, but you can be sure the Goblins are going to try it."

"Dammit." She shook her head. Their left side was the weak point in their defense. The Goblins had now gotten a good look at their position and would move to exploit any weakness they could find. "Can they get around behind us?"

"Not that I could tell. From down there, if you kept on toward our rear, the slope just goes further down." He brushed rain away from his eyes absently. "There might be a way to get back on the road behind us, but if there is, it won't be quick or easy. My guess is, they will have to try to charge up this hill." He gestured to the nearly forty-five-degree slope in front of them.

"You've told Ortran what you saw?"

"Yeah. He's putting an extra spearman along the edge here."

"I guess that's all we can do." She arched her shoulders back to keep loose.

"Would you care for a shield, miss?" An Ialish soldier offered her the iron-plated shield of one of his fallen comrades.

"I'll keep it handy, thanks." Her preferred combat techniques did not allow for shield use, but if Goblin archers somehow managed to get a bead on them, she'd be glad to have it around.

"Sir?" The soldier extended his offer to Resaka. Lena read his face as he was about to politely refuse. She arched an eyebrow and gestured with her bow. Resaka reluctantly accepted the offer.

"Let's watch ourselves," she spoke to her fellows that were positioned on the left flank. "If they put archers down there, Ortran may order us to go down and dig them out."

"Well said," the competitive Ialu beside her spoke. "My name is Betov." He nodded to her and Resaka. "I'd estimate at this range with their small bows shooting uphill through the leaves and the rain; their arrows would have little effect against our steel." He proudly clanged the short shaft of his long-bladed spear against his chest plate. "Plus, they would have to stop shooting to let their brothers assail the hill."

"Let's hope you're right," Resaka interjected. "I'm happy to stay up here for the duration of the battle." Lena looked up sharply as the sound of the Goblin battle horns sounded once again through the ravine.

"That didn't take long," Lena commented. "Try to stay awake, Betov," She joked with the Ialu in front of her.

"I'll do my best, miss," he answered with a slight tip of his helm. They stood in a tense stillness as the Goblin charge grew closer. Ortran had decided to forgo the initial archery barrages this round. They would have little effect on the total number of Goblin casualties, and breaking formation to allow a group of archers through the line at the last moment posed a needless risk. Best to save their arrows for short-range shots that had specific tactical benefits. Lena had set her bow aside and stood ready with her broadsword in hand. With the assumed ferocity of the incoming attack, Lena felt her sword would have more work to do than her bow. The newly acquired shield felt awkward on her left arm, but the sense of security it brought was more than welcome. Ortran, Hagen, and the injured soldier were all mounted to give them a better vantage point to fire arrows. Maco had been armed with a bow as well.

The Goblins surged around the corner as before, bellowing and shrieking with crazed savagery. The Ialu stood fast and received their charge like a boulder in the crashing surf. The man on the left corner was targeted specifically, and if not for the fellow directly behind him holding fast to his armor, he would have been swept over the side immediately. The spearmen began their grisly work in unison, churning their weapons forward, methodically reaping Goblin lives in a hideous display.

For a moment, the Goblin charge seemed to be halted in its tracks. Lena stood by, gripped by a paralyzing feeling of uselessness as the Goblins smashed themselves heedlessly against the Ialu shield wall. The Ialu had grown wise to the Goblin tactic of launching their fellows into the air to crash down on the line from above. Several times a Goblin body soared into the air toward the Ialish line, and each time he was intercepted by at least one arrow and disappeared back into the maelstrom of violence.

Time distorts itself in battle. Each moment can ooze by in exquisite slowness, while simultaneously, the entire experience can seem to vanish in an instantaneous blur. Lena could not clearly discern how long the battle raged or accurately determine the casualty rate or tactical position for either side – all that was tangible was the feel of it. The crushing weight of death in the air, swirling around them like a ghost in a storm. The Goblins fell like the rain that pounded them all while the blood and water churned the road into a hideous mire. A steady stream of straggling Goblins would fall over the side and scramble to gain a hold to the meager foliage there, only to either lose footing in the mud and be swept away downhill or to struggle up the slope and be slaughtered by Ialish spears.

Lena snapped into sharp focus as a stone the size of a brick fell from directly above, striking a glancing blow off Betov's shoulder guard. She whipped her head around, scanning the ridgeline above. A line of Goblins, darkened silhouettes against the grey sky, stood on the ridge top, hurling large rocks down at them from their vantage point, roughly three stories above. More large stones began to fall amongst the hard-pressed Ialu, striking one fellow directly on the top of his helm, dropping him like a sack of grain.

"Shields overhead!" Ortran bellowed. The few Ialu who were not directly engaged with the Goblin onslaught raised their shields overhead, attempting to protect as many of their fellows as possible. Still, they were too few to cover their ranks in the front who were desperately fending off the maniacal attack.

"Pevma!" Lena shouted, pointing to the new threat. Tossing her shield aside, Lena snatched her bow from her shoulder and struggled to thread an arrow on the wet string. Ortran and the other archers turned their attention upward and began to shoot, but at such an angle and in the rain, their arrows had little effect. A few shafts streaked harmlessly into the air or caromed off of the stone face of the hillside. Pevma shouted something indiscernible and gestured with both arms as if tossing an invisible object skyward. For a moment, the Goblins on the hilltop above them continued to hurl down stones, ignoring the arrows among their ranks. The next moment, a brilliant ball of unearthly fire burst forth in the trees and shrubs all around the Goblins. Their shrieks of pain and fear were audible even above the din of the battle below, and they scattered immediately. Some fell, though luckily, missing the Ialu soldiers below. The fire burned brightly, shedding an unnaturally bluish tint, as it stormed from branch to branch on the hilltop.

"In this rain, that won't last long," Pevma warned. Already the fire began to dim, though there was no further sign of Goblins in the midst of it.

"Well, at least now they know we have a mage," Ortran shouted, struggling to control his mount as it danced nervously beneath him. "Perhaps the fear of that alone will discourage them." Lena could only hope he was right. The raging battle in the front slacked for a moment, and Lena briefly held the hope that the Goblins had lost heart. Ortran's reaction shattered her hopes. "Left corner! Watch…" His shouted warning was cut short as three of the Ialu holding the forward left corner of the line were simultaneously swept aside and down into the ravine. Betov and two others tumbled down into the foliage and were lost to sight almost immediately. A fourth was knocked flat on his back and trampled into the mud as a charge broke through the Ialu ranks.

The Goblins had brought forth a trunk section from a medium-sized tree and driven it like a battering ram into the Ialish line. The Goblins bearing the makeshift ram were larger than most, large enough to have maneuvered the weapon along the road and charge forward with their burden. They dropped the ram on the road in the midst of the Ialu formation, pulling crudely-forged, curved blades from their belts and lunging into the now exposed flank of the line of spearmen. Without hesitation, Lena threw her bow aside and leapt onto the log, broadsword in hand.

The closest Goblin was nearly as tall as she was. He shifted his footing and turned immediately toward her drawing his blade back to deliver a sweeping slash. Her rapid thrust to his midsection caught him before he could complete his attack, and his body fell over the edge as she lifted the hilt of her sword to pitch him sideways into the ravine.

The Ialu formation reacted quickly to the new attackers, dividing their attention between the front line and the new threat. A spear surged forward, distracting the next Goblin long enough for Lena to remove his head. Another of the large Goblins sprang forward with a heavy downward chop. Lena caught the attack with her blade held horizontally overhead, turning her body and diverting the force of the strike downward and away to her left, placing the Goblin between herself and the ravine. She lunged forward, stepping inside of the effective range of both of their blades, and pushed against his body with the hilt of her weapon, driving the protruding end of the cross-shaped guard into her opponent's sternum. He stumbled backward, catching a heel on the wet log behind him, and pitched rearward over the edge of the ravine with a startled yelp.

She heard Ortran shouting commands in Ialish as she faced off with the last two of the large Goblins who had gained their flank. One was immediately sent over the edge by a brutal shield bash from an Ialish soldier. The moment's distraction was all she needed to stab the final fellow. Her blade caught him in the left shoulder as he raised his own guard a moment too late. He rolled away, attempting to mitigate the force of her blow, exposing his right side to the Ialish soldiers. A vicious spear thrust from the Ialu beside her ended him, and he fell back into the ravine below. A spearman brought his shield to bear and stepped forward to complete the shield wall once again. The Ialu line pressed forward, forcing the Goblins back toward the bend in the road, inching forward one labored step at a time.

Lena marveled at the incredible strength necessary to not only fend off the tidal wave of snarling enemies but to drive them back along the muddy road. With the grinding force of a sliding boulder, the formation slowly drove the Goblins back past the fallen log, effectively sealing up the hole that had been created. Several Ialu had fallen in the chaotic exchange and were dragged clear of the fray by Burkus and the professor. Lena shot a look over the edge toward the three soldiers who had tumbled over the rim. She could hear shouts and clanging of weapons from below.

"Ortran!" Resaka shouted, holding up a rope. He had fastened one end to the log and gestured over the edge toward their fallen comrades. Ortran spared them a quick glance and nodded. Resaka turned toward the slope and tossed the rope over the edge. "Shall we?" He gestured to the edge as if inviting her for an evening carriage ride.

"You're insane," she commented with a shake of her head. She took the rope in one hand, and with her sword in the other, she half descended, half fell down the slope crashing through the small saplings and brambles that clung to the steep ground. She lost her footing in the thickening mud and outright tumbled the last few paces, miraculously maintaining a grip on her sword and managing not to slice herself in the process. As she struggled to her feet, Resaka came crashing in a heap beside her, sliding on his rear through the mud with one hand somehow still on the wet rope.

The three Ialu soldiers had regained their footing in time to face a troop of Goblins who had slunk across the valley floor as the battle raged on above. They flailed about with their larger weapons, abandoning their short-bladed swords in favor of heavy axes and hammers. Quite a few Goblins lay motionless on the forest floor, some clearly had fallen from above, and some had been felled in this smaller skirmish that she and Resaka had just stumbled into.

Without a word, Lena charged forward to engage the Goblins. There were at least ten that she could count, though Vochny's warning of unseen foes echoed in her ears. Resaka whipped his heavy saber from his hip and threw himself into the fray, slashing his blade in a blur of motion. Lena recalled from their experience at the fencing academy that what Resaka lacked in finesse, he made up for with pure speed. Master Garis had given him the nickname "lightning," and the Goblins were learning the hard way how he had earned such a title.

She focused her attention on the Goblins that were moving to engage with her. She planted her feet as the first Goblin closed with her. Without slowing, he chopped toward her midsection with a black iron short sword. She lifted the hilt of

94

her sword, keeping the point low, and deflected the attack off to her side, her blade held close to her body. She stepped forward, allowing the force of the Goblin's charge to take him past her as she whipped the handle of her weapon in a tight circle above her head.

Her foe lost balance, stumbling as he drove his weight against a person who was no longer there. She drew her blade in a vicious downward cut across his exposed back, sending him sprawling to the forest floor. The second Goblin rushing toward her tried to check his forward movement lest he run right past Lena and over his fallen comrade. She turned her sword and pivoted the motion of her blade to attack in an upward slash toward the Goblin's throat as he balked. He managed to bring his crude stone-headed mace to bear and intercept the attack in time to keep his own head attached, but the force of Lena's blow drove the handle of his weapon against his body, bearing him over onto his back as he slipped in the wet leaves on the forest floor.

The combat at the foot of the hill was more spread out and chaotic than the tightly pressed formation at the top. Goblins raced around loosely and without clear strategy aside from a vicious desire to kill their foes. The clamor of colliding weaponry and shrieking Goblin voices from above was clearly audible even from a distance and over the clanging battle and rainfall here below. A headless Goblin body from the combat above crashed to the ground between Lena and her foe, allowing Lena's opponent time to scurry to his feet, dropping several steps backward.

"Glad you could join us," Betov commented as the Goblin he faced crumpled into a lifeless heap from a downward hammer blow.

"No trouble," she responded tersely. "I wasn't busy." Their conversation was cut short as a pair of Goblins darted forward, one closed with Betov and the other engaged Lena with an iron-tipped spear. Without hesitation, he thrust his spear at her face, snarling angrily. She batted the attack aside with the flat of her sword and immediately stepped forward to stab toward his center, now that her blade was inside his guard. This Goblin, however, seemed a bit more in control of himself than some of his fellows. He checked his forward motion and stepped back, sweeping the length of his spear in front of him to divert her attack. He continued his backward movement, drawing the spear back with his rear hand. Lena pressed her momentum and moved with him. An opponent with a spear had superior reach, and she wanted to stay close to deny her foe that advantage.

Just as his rear foot planted in the soft earth behind him, he thrust forward again, aiming his spear toward her lead leg as she shifted her weight forward. Unable to check her momentum quickly enough to step aside, she managed to drop her blade in a low sweeping motion to divert his attack away to her right, but his spear glanced off of the shin guard of her rear leg. She pivoted her sword and drove forward in a stabbing motion toward his belly, now that they were close. The Goblin lifted his back hand, sweeping the haft of the spear across in front of his body, barely diverting her thrust away from his torso with the center of his weapon as he twisted in place. Lena continued her forward driving motion and crashed into her opponent with her hip and shoulder. Having lifted his weight to shift and pivot his body, he lacked stable footing, and with her hip, she drove him back and off of his feet. She closed quickly and pinned him to the wet earth before he could regain his footing. His scream was still in the air when another of his fellows leapt forward to attack.

His face was painted with vertical white lines and twisted with rage as he closed in at nearly a full run. He was taller than his fellows but exceedingly lanky and brandished what was little more than a sharp-looking rock tied to the end of a thick stick. He growled something in his own language and smashed heavily toward Lena's head with a straight overhead attack right along his center. She jerked her blade free from her previous opponent's body and swept it across in front of her torso as she stepped back to gain a proper distance for combat. She deflected the chopping motion of his makeshift axe, but instead of planting his feet for his next maneuver, the Goblin abandoned his weapon entirely and leapt forward with his arms outstretched in a tackling motion. The timing and speed of the Goblin's rush caught her as she was shifting her balance to her rear foot. If she had been rooted more firmly, she would have been able to bring her sword up solidly and end the fight immediately, but she was caught off guard with his unorthodox tactic, and the Goblin managed to grab hold of her iron shoulder guards and bear them both to the ground.

Lena landed flat on her back with her sword hilt and both hands pinned between herself and her opponent. She was unable to bring it to bear with his weight pressing her arms flat against her, but he could not gain any leverage to do anything further without lifting his chest off of her arms and therefore freeing her. As they both scrambled to gain the advantage, the Goblin wiggled his left hand to grab her left forearm and lift himself upward, pressing down with his weight in an attempt to keep her weapon pinned.

His right hand shot to his hip and whipped a crude iron stiletto from his belt. Lena's arm was twisted across her body at an awkward angle, making it impossible to wrench free quickly enough to avoid the imminent downward stab. With strength borne of desperation, she heaved her hip upward, lifting her right thigh to dislodge the Goblin. He pitched forward, and his stabbing action became a desperate flailing motion to avoid tumbling face-first into the mud. With the Goblin's weight now nearly completely diverted onto his right elbow, he chose to abandon grappling and regain his footing before she was able to toss him aside completely and bring her weapon to bear. He rolled away, sliding in the mud as they both struggled to their feet. Lena whipped her sword to a guard position and faced off with her opponent, who was now armed only with a short stabbing knife. Her opponent dropped like a stone as Betov's hammer pounded his skull from behind.

She had only time to nod in thanks before running footsteps across the muddy forest floor behind her caught her attention. She spun immediately and, by instinct alone, diverted a vicious sword slash from a short, thick Goblin. With a short, wide-bladed sword in each hand, he rolled one attack after another, driving forward in a whirlwind of slashing iron. Lena paced backward, giving ground and swatting attacks aside as she struggled to regain firm footing on the muddy ground. The Goblin pressed forward relentlessly, hoping to keep Lena off balance long enough to score a hit.

She felt a thin tree branch pressing across her back as she retreated, the pressure slowly increasing as the green sapling bowed against her passing. She bent at the waist suddenly, allowing the branch to whip forward over her body and spring fully into the Goblin's face. Lunging forward instantly, she stabbed the Goblin in the belly as he struggled unexpectedly against his new foe, the tree. He bellowed loudly and stumbled backward, dropping one sword to clutch at his wound. Lena pressed her attack, returning slashes in the same fashion she had received them, relentlessly rolling one attack after another. Facing the longer reach of her broadsword, the Goblin had little chance to counter, and he began to give ground more quickly, scrambling backward in an attempt to gain enough space to break and run.

Another Goblin body crashed through the foliage from above, distracting Lena just enough for her opponent to turn and dart away. She was happy to let him flee. It was not necessary (nor likely possible) for them to finish every Goblin that faced them. All that was needed was to inflict sufficient injury that the Goblins felt the cost of continuing the fight was more than the value of whatever Xedrin's man had promised them – hoping, of course, that the Goblins were not motivated by something greater than greed. Hatred can drive a people to commit themselves to complete self-destruction despite any logical arguments to the contrary.

Lena panned her gaze rapidly around the combat area. One Ialu was down, his body being savaged by four Goblins where it fell. Betov and Resaka had fallen in beside each other and were holding their own against a crowd of Goblin raiders. Resaka's blade flashed in a near blur, keeping the shorter limbed Goblins at bay for the moment. Betov whirled his hammer in tight circles above his head, and judging by the ring of fallen Goblins around them, Lena could understand why the ones they faced were growing hesitant to rush in. The last Ialu was being pressed hard by four enemies, their blows heavily ringing off his shield and armor as he flailed with his axe. He was clearly dazed by the barrage of strikes against his body, and it seemed a matter of moments before a Goblin was able to score a solid hit and end the fight. Lena spurred forward, rushing to lend aid as a bright flash of bluish light from above blasted through the forest. The Goblins all balked, glancing around nervously, as a thunderous boom followed on the heels of the flash. Resaka took advantage of the distraction to relieve a Goblin of his head.

Lena shouted and skidded to a halt beside the injured Ialu, bringing her sword up just as a series of short horn blasts echoed through the ravine. The Goblins all turned and ran simultaneously, disappearing into the forest in almost an instant.

The Ialu beside her dropped to one knee, panting heavily and shaking his head. She cautiously scanned the woods, looking for signs of their enemy in case the retreat was merely a ruse. The leaves grew still as the sounds of the battle above faded. Lena could hear Ortran's voice shouting orders from the road above.

"Ha," Resaka taunted half-heartedly. "Bunch of quitters." He panted heavily, leaning forward to catch his breath. Betov turned to check on their fallen comrade as Lena lifted her gaze to survey the distance. On a ridge across the gorge from the Ialish position on the road, Lena could just make out a column of Goblins moving around toward the rear of the Ialu held ground. It would take the Goblins some time to navigate back to the road from across the ravine, but as she watched the stream of Goblins charging across the far hill, she knew their numbers would be sufficient to finish the Ialu completely.

"We gotta get out of here." She pointed with her sword at the newest threat. "Now." She moved to lend a hand to the injured Ialu beside her. It was a sign of the extent of his injury that he allowed it without a word.

"Hurkta is dead," Betov announced. "Alcher, can you make it back up the hill?" he asked. Alcher simply nodded and stumbled forward toward the incline. One by one, they struggled up the rope that Resaka had left behind. Betov and Resaka fought to assist Alcher up the rope as Lena stayed behind to guard their rear. She was the last to gain the ridge, the muscles in her hands and forearms burning as she grappled with the muddy rope. As she gained her footing on the road, the scene that lay before her caught her breath.

Of the twenty soldiers that had accompanied Ortran from Rafa, only nine remained. Ortran and Maco brought the Ialish company to eleven. The professor and Burkus both still lived, though Burkus seemed to be favoring a wound to his left arm. Pevma was seated on the blood-soaked ground, her hands splayed out on the ground in front of her. She leaned forward and hung her head low. For a moment, Lena feared the worst. She rushed to the other woman's side.

"I'm all right," she said weakly. "That last spell just took a lot out of me." Lena helped the Selyr to her feet and looked around. Three of the velni horses were also down, but most of their mounts were still unharmed, tethered in place along the road behind them.

A sea of Goblin dead covered the road. Far too many bodies to count lay churned into the mud, their weapons and lifeless limbs jutting out of the hideous mire like miniature broken trees after a firestorm. The rain fell unabated, thickening the churned-up earth of the road into a nearly impassible quagmire. Fat drops of rain hissed as they fell among the dying remnants of the unnatural fire still burning in the low foliage around the path. Ortran surveyed the field with a deep grimace, one blood-soaked hand stroking his chin absently. Betov closed with his commander and delivered his report, gesturing to the far ridge. Ortran nodded grimly.

"Our position is lost," he announced. "We will break and ride like mad for the river."

"What of our dead, sir?" Vochny asked. Ortran ground his teeth with frustration.

"I fear we must leave them," came the reply. Vochny's eyes spoke the words he could not say. The idea of leaving their brave fallen to be savaged by the Goblins was abhorrent to the Ialu, but there was little option.

Ortran spent a few moments of their dwindling time to arrange their fallen in a line along the side of the road. A long tarp was draped over their bodies, with the hope that the Goblins may overlook the makeshift grave in their haste. Lena glanced nervously over her shoulder as the surviving Ialu removed their helms, and Ortran spoke some quick words in Ialish. The Ialish soldiers turned and solemnly went about the business of breaking their position and preparing the horses.

"Vedok Ortran," Lena spoke to the Ialish commander. "I saw at least three distinctly different looking kinds of Goblin warriors down there. Are we facing multiple tribes?"

"I believe so," he responded. "I observed the same up here."

"I haven't fought Goblins before," she admitted. "From what I've heard, though, it seems unusual."

"It is, though not unheard of." Ortran ushered Lena to the edge of the road. "You see this big fellow?" He indicated one of the larger Goblins who had borne the makeshift battering ram. "The paint on his face suggests he's from the high mountains further north."

"Is that why he is so much bigger than the rest?"

"His size? No. Goblins are unique in that they never quite stop growing." He pointed at another Goblin, one of a more expected stature. "Upon reaching adulthood, a Goblin is about so large. Most Goblins you see are of that size. They do, however, continue to grow, although much more slowly as they age. A Goblin in his golden years may be nearly as tall as a human."

"These fellows don't look all that old, though." Lena tilted her head toward the large, northern Goblins.

"Ah yes, that is where we wander into the unknown." Ortran paused to issue a command to one of his soldiers in Ialish. "It is said that Goblin leaders will challenge each other to personal combat for control of the village. The winner will enter the tent of the shaman to eat the loser's heart and be bathed in his blood with the smoke of a sacred herb. Supposedly the ritual imbues the Goblins with greater size and strength than they would ever gain on their own."

"I see." Lena suppressed an involuntary shudder. "So, these northern fellows were of high standing in their tribe."

"Indeed. The war leaders of villages and tribes will have won many battles amongst each other for control. As they consume the power of each of their rivals, they grow all the more. A Goblin king could be the size of a Troll."

"That big?"

"I've seen it myself." Ortran nodded. "Now, I'm not sure I believe all the talk of eating hearts, but there is certainly *something* going on." Ortran excused himself for another moment as he gave additional orders to his men. The soldiers were moving the Goblin dead into a large pile in the center of the path as if they meant to block the road with a grisly makeshift wall. Lena observed with a grimace that there were likely enough bodies to do the job rather effectively.

"Might I ask?" She gestured to the soldiers performing their unpleasant task.

"You have seen that a Goblin's chief weapon is their passion." Ortran paused to wipe the rain from his eyes. "The will of their king unites them. Drives them onward. It is his will, and his will alone, that keeps these tribes together – whips them up into such a bloody frenzy. These disparate tribes would never stand beside each other without a great king to make it so. As much as I detest desecrating the bodies of an enemy, even one who would show us no such respect, tools such as this are an effective way to counter his will." As the last of the hideous wall was completed, Pevma closed her eyes and began to utter a spell. A cloud of bluish-grey smoke began to rise from the pile of corpses, defying the rain with an unnatural will of its own.

"This little show should put a dent in their self-confidence. When they finally screw up enough courage to come at us a fourth time, they will have to claw their way through that horrific mess, and in doing so, the seeds of doubt are planted. They will begin to question if their king truly can lead them to victory. The next time they face us, the vision of their dead cousins will be fresh on their minds, and they will fight with half a heart."

"The smoke is a nice touch," Lena added.

"Our friend Pevma suggested as much." Ortran nodded to the Selyr as she wearily mounted her horse. "I trust it will be worth the delay." He glanced at the sky. "We are in a race against the sun now. We ride!" he finished loudly. With no further fanfare, the soldiers mounted their horses and rocketed away down the road.

* * * * *

Lena forced herself to her feet and handed the water flask to Resaka. He gulped the water down as fast as he could between ragged breaths, making no effort to conceal his exertion. The flight to the river had been a desperate surge – a nightmarish blur of winding muddy road switching back on itself countless times until the pounding of Steel's hooves over the path became the only thing that felt real. The sound of Goblin battle horns repeatedly echoed through the narrow valleys, making it nearly impossible to tell where the enemy was or how close they were. As they charged along the road, arrows would streak unexpectedly from the darkening woods, more often than not to be either deflected by the superior Ialish armor or to simply miss their target completely. Some found their mark, however; one Ialish soldier was lost, and another two were wounded. Two more of their stout velni horses had fallen as well. Ortran himself took a barrage of arrows across his back as he paused to survey the road behind them; most were deflected, but one shaft slipped through a seam on his left shoulder, inflicting a minor wound.

The company had somehow managed to outpace the Goblins for the moment, and they paused by the river to take a much-needed rest. The road broke through the tree line three hundred or so paces away from the riverbank and assaulted a slight rise, leading to a narrow wooden bridge. The riverbanks here were steep, nearly vertical, and plunged fifty paces nearly straight down into a raging torrent of floodwater. Ortran had been confident that this bridge was the only useable crossing for leagues in either direction. About a league past the bridge on the opposite bank, the terrain flattened out significantly, and the road became broad and straight. The hope had been to gain the flat road before nightfall, and once they were able to fully take advantage of their superior mounted speed, they could outpace the Goblins and simply ride to safety. As they paused to water their mounts, it became clear that the final stretch of winding road would be too long.

"We won't make it." Ortran glowered. "It's too dark to charge headlong through this mire." He gestured to the failing sunlight. "We'd simply be doing the Goblins a favor by killing ourselves."

"You don't think it's worth a try?" Lena asked, stomping her feet to stimulate circulation in her numb legs.

"I've traveled this road a few times," Ortran responded grimly. "Across the bank, the path becomes much more treacherous. Very steep. It's tricky to ride at a walk on dry ground in the full sun." He wiped the sweat from his brow and winced in pain from his wound. "With a horde of Goblins nipping at our heels, we'd be doomed. Better to turn and face them here at the bridge where we can put up a good fight."

"At least we've got room for a decent cavalry charge." Lena surveyed the open ground between the river and the tree line. Running horses over uneven ground through the mud in the dark was likely a recipe for disaster, but even without the benefit of a proper charge, fighting from horseback lent itself several distinct advantages. Resaka handed the water flask back to Lena.

"Maybe I'm overstepping here, but why don't we burn down the bridge?" he asked. "That should keep them off our butts long enough for us to get down the mountain."

"I like the way you think, Mister Devaash, but the wood is too wet. Damn this rain." Ortran chuckled halfheartedly.

"Well, it was a thought. What's our play, then?" he asked, glancing between Lena and Ortran.

"I will position a group on the bridge," Ortran began. "Burkus and the Professor have agreed to stay close and protect Maco as best they can. Pevma has chosen to stand with them as well. Alcher and Hagen are both wounded; unfit to man a shield wall. I'll have them with bows on either side of the bridge. That leaves Urzbek, Betov, and Vochny to form a line. I plan to stay mounted with my three remaining soldiers. We will wreak as much havoc as we can on horseback in the failing light and then fall back to the wall and raise spears."

"Sounds good enough." Resaka nodded.

"I won't exceed my authority and order either of you to do anything, but any help you can offer is appreciated," Ortran added.

"I'm useless fighting from a horse," Resaka admitted. "I can take a spear and back your guys up at the bridge until it's time for sword work." He unconsciously ran his hand across a bandage over a leg wound he could not remember receiving.

"I've got some experience with cavalry," Lena stated. "I'll join you on the field if you'll have me."

"Now, a word of caution before you commit," Ortran warned. "It is likely that the Goblin King will show his face this time. It would be a display of power for him over his people to strike a blow against me personally. If we see him, I plan to make a line straight for him."

"We won't have time or the manpower to guard our rear or our flanks," Lena observed. "That would be a one-way charge."

"I am afraid so," Ortran agreed. "If I can kill the king, their morale would shatter." He smacked a fist into his palm. "The remaining Goblins will scatter into the trees."

"And if he kills you…" Lena started.

"Then one of you needs to kill him."

"That's quite a gamble," Resaka added.

"Likely, we are all dead anyway," Ortran responded grimly.

"True." Resaka forced a grin.

"I'm in. Taking the king is our best hope," Lena stated, peering into the darkening forest. "They are going to be here any moment. We should be getting ready."

"You have my thanks, Miss Sullivan," Ortran said with a stiff bow. "My gratitude, Mister Devaash." He turned away and approached the bridge to arrange his men according to his plan.

"You sure about riding out there?" Resaka asked as he adjusted the straps of his armor. "You guys are going to get surrounded pretty quick."

"Taking the Goblin King is the only way we make it out of here alive," she answered. "I don't fancy putting myself in the middle of a field surrounded by Goblins, but I don't see another way to win this one."

"Are we sure the Goblins will run if we manage to take out the chief?" Resaka asked, inspecting the edge of his saber. "Suppose they just get extra upset and feel like venting their frustration on us?"

"Well, there aren't any guarantees, clearly," Lena admitted. "But what Ortran is saying matches what I've heard in everywhere else." Lena brushed Steel's shoulder. "Goblin tribes are only held together by a firm authority. It's what drives them. Once that is lost, coupled with the catastrophic losses we have already inflicted, it's a safe bet they will turn and run."

"Safe or not, looks like it's our only bet."

"There's that too," she admitted.

"As long as we're betting, I'd bet that their chief is aware of such a strategy," Resaka suggested.

"Yeah. Probably," Lena agreed. "It won't be easy to get to him, and judging by the size of the group he's managed to put together, he is going to be a tough one himself."

"Worth a shot anyway." Resaka spun his sword absently, rotating his shoulder and wrist to loosen up. A Goblin battle horn sounded in the forest. He shot a look toward the trees. "At least we won't get bored waiting." He turned back to Lena.

"So…" He met her eyes. There was always warmth in his gaze. He paused as if struggling to say more. "I'm glad we were friends," he started.

"We aren't dead yet."

"Well, *I'm* not." He chuckled. "You're in trouble, though." He absently stroked Steel's neck. "Get on that horse and show these Ialish chaps what proper cavalry looks like." He stepped back and shuffled his feet unconsciously. Lena shook her head. And men said that women were the emotional ones. She stepped into the stirrup and swung easily into the saddle.

"I'm glad we were friends too," she added. "You can buy this friend some whiskey in Nephron once we get there."

"Fair enough." He turned to walk toward the bridge. "Save some Goblins for the rest of us," he shot over his shoulder.

"No promises," she answered, spurring Steel to a trot. Another horn sounded, this time much closer. She could see indistinct movement in the deepening shadows just beyond the tree line. She rode up beside her Ialish companions.

"Well, Miss Sullivan, our reckoning has come," Ortran said. He pointed with his spear across the field. "I hope to keep our horses within that high spot in the center. Let them come to us. Off to either side, the ground is too soft for cavalry."

"Understood." She nodded. Steel danced eagerly as the energy of the approaching battle began to rise. He was a large animal, aggressive, and trained for combat. More than a few Goblins would fall beneath his hooves. A final horn sounded just within the trees, and a wave of Goblins burst from the shadows. The mud slowed their charge in some places, and their line fell into disarray almost immediately.

Ortran sat patiently on his horse as he observed the field, his spear held aloft, waiting to choose his target. Lena reined Steel back as she felt his aggression growing. She watched as the group of Goblins running across the drier, center ground began to outpace their brothers, who lagged behind as they struggled through the mud.

"On my mark, we charge those hapless bastards in the middle. Strike the first few lines, then heel left and circle back." Lena watched the Goblins charging across the field for a tense moment. She felt her mind sliding into the single-mindedness of combat, welcoming the cool insulation of mental detachment from the natural fear that threatened to swallow her. "NOW!" Ortran leveled his spear and spurred his horse forward. Lena kicked Steel into action but immediately found herself pulling him back slightly lest he outpace the smaller velni horses. They needed to strike as a group. She charged forward, Steel's hooves hungrily devouring the ground between him and his foes. The two lines came together with a clatter, and in the blink of an eye, she and her companions had left well over a half-dozen Goblins face down in the mud. She let Steel have his way as he churned back up the hill, arriving a moment before the Ialu soldiers. The

Goblins bellowed furiously and continued unabated, running recklessly toward their position.

"Again. This time break right," Ortran ordered. "Charge!" Again, they plunged through their foes like a knife through butter. Afoot and on the move, with no significant pole weapons amongst them, the Goblins stood little chance against the charging horses. The cavalry mowed down more of their foes without a single wound amongst themselves. Once again, Lena regained the hilltop before her companions.

"What do you think?" she shouted. "One more?" The Goblins had nearly crossed the useable portion of the field, though, at the moment, they were spread out more thinly than she had feared. Ortran nodded.

"Last one, then we hold the center. Keep a tight circle as long as we can." On his order, they charged a third time, chewing through their enemies as before. The Goblin formation had deteriorated from a line into a loose mass of frenetic movement. Goblins ran in seemingly random directions as small groups formed, each with their own strategy. Lena could hear her companions on the bridge engage the enemy; the sound of weapons clashing against metal and the screams of dying Goblin warriors from the bridge could be heard above the thundering of hooves and screams beside her. The enemy now held the entire field.

Instead of veering off after the initial clash, she and her fellow cavalry soldiers kept plowing forward to reach a wider space of slightly dryer ground in the center of the field. With foes spread loosely around on every side, charge tactics were now unfeasible. In the lead, Ortran veered his horse to the left as the other animals fell in single file behind him and began to move in a tight circle. With their right side open to the enemy, they were open to use their weapons as freely as possible and still utilize the speed and power of their mounts.

Lena's sword rose and fell, sweeping into the mass of foes repeatedly. The shorter stature of the Goblin raiders proved to be a disadvantage to both sides of this conflict. A Goblin without a long weapon stood little chance of reaching a mounted opponent, and likewise, for Lena to effectively engage her foes, she needed to lean over significantly more than she was accustomed to, compromising her effectiveness. Within moments, the cavalry and Goblins fell into a stalemate. Any

Goblins foolish enough to rush forward were either immediately trampled or cut down, but any pause in motion from the horses would result in that rider being swarmed from all sides. An arrow whizzed by Lena's cheek, distracting her long enough for the target of her sword slash to roll away unharmed.

"Archers!" she shouted in warning. Another arrow streaked past. While Goblin archers had thus far proven themselves to be somewhat lacking in both effective equipment and skill, if she and her companions continued to simply ride in circles, the bowmen would have ample opportunity for practice. As if to punctuate her thought, an arrow lodged itself firmly into her right saddlebag, striking a fatal wound to her canvas field tent. Steel snorted in response to the unexpected slap on his rump and nearly bucked.

"Dammit! Break!" Ortran ordered. Each of the horses immediately broke to their right, charging in a straight line from the circle's center. The Goblins in front of her panicked in response to the unexpected maneuver, and Steel trampled two immediately as Lena clove the skull of a third. Without the safety of a closed circle to her left, Lena needed to wheel her mount around constantly, dropping her blade back and forth to either side to defend both flanks. The other horsemen thrashed about in a similar fashion, leaving a trail of fallen Goblins in their wake. For a moment, Lena felt hope. If she and her companions could maintain the momentum and initiative, maybe...

Her thought was cut short as a mass of synchronized movement to her left caught her attention. A dozen Goblins all charged forward together and simultaneously launched a barrage of iron-tipped javelins. The volley of missiles blanketed an Ialu horseman, piercing him and his mount several times. They went down in a tangle of flailing limbs and were immediately swarmed by Goblin footmen. A large Goblin, seemingly the leader of the javelin brigade, turned and pointed to Lena, shouting orders. The troop scrambled to adjust their position, moving to face her in a line where they could shower her with spears as they had her companion.

Without hesitation, Lena spurred Steel forward to rush their position, hoping to close the distance before they could ready their weapons. She closed with them just as they had formed a line, slashing her weapon down in a short arc, sending one Goblin sprawling. Another leapt aside to avoid being trampled. While she had broken their formation for the moment, her forward momentum was taking her too far away from them to repeat her tactic before they had their weapons ready to throw. She urged Steel forward still, hoping to exceed their effective throwing range before she and her horse were pierced by the next wave of javelins.

Not daring to look behind, Lena focused her energy on maneuvering between the Goblins in front of her, as some either dove aside or rushed to engage. The battle had deteriorated into a chaotic frenzy; neither side had any discernable formation nor held any specific ground.

The light had almost faded completely, and with the still overcast sky, the field was nearly black as tar. She could barely see far enough in front of Steel to avoid charging him into an extended spear or even a tree. His front hoof caught in the mud, and he stumbled, his forelegs making sucking sounds as he struggled through an unexpectedly deep patch of mud. Riding like this would kill him faster than the Goblins would.

With an eloquent curse, she leapt from the saddle and slapped Steel on the rump. He would know to run to safety, and likely as not, the Goblins would have no motivation to try to stop him. She took two powerful strides forward and lopped an arm off the closest Goblin before he could react. An instant later, a volley of javelins rained down on the earth where she had dismounted only a moment ago, killing one of their own. She batted aside an outstretched blade and drove forward, hoping to extract herself from the muddy lower ground before her opponents could overwhelm her.

The key to surviving an engagement such as this was constant movement. With no one to guard her back or flanks and enemies all around, to take a firm position would be an invitation for the Goblins to swarm her. She churned up the slight rise, shouldering a Goblin aside as she parried an attack from his companion. Lena was no longer trying to defeat any single opponent in combat. She was simply trying to survive. In the near-total darkness, Lena found that none but the few Goblins in her immediate vicinity were aware of her. As long as she kept moving, the Goblin horde as a whole had no idea where she was specifically and could not direct a coordinated attack against her.

Unfortunately, the same was not true for her companions defending the bridge. Lena could see the faint silhouette of the Ialu soldiers at the top of the rise, struggling to ward off the flood of enemies that faced them. Goblin soldiers ran past her screaming, hell-bent on attacking their despised enemy at the top of the hill, looking forward to the spilling of blood, whether it be Ialish or their own. The pure animal hatred in their eyes was simultaneously unsettling and astonishing. She had no way to know how the remainder of the small cavalry troop had fared nor how to connect with them to coordinate their own efforts. She was seemingly lost in a sea of swirling weapons, snarling faces, rain, mud, and blood.

She lashed out at a tall Goblin, bearing him back against one of his fellows. Without waiting for his countermove, she turned and stepped forward to catch a Goblin's weapon arm with her left hand, stopping his motion before it began. She wrenched him aside, tossing him to the ground, and stepped forward again to parry a blade suddenly slashing at her from the darkness. This was sheer madness. She had to unite with her fellows, or she would be overwhelmed by this mob in moments. Lena drove forward, hoping to move back toward the bridge, stabbing a Goblin through the middle as she painfully absorbed a club smash from another with nothing but the armor of her left arm. She panted heavily as she pushed back up the hill, carving a path through her enemies. She was expending far too much energy far too quickly, and at this rate, she feared that even if she was able to regain the hill, she would be spent and unable to defend it.

She grunted as she fell to one knee, slipping in the mud. A weapon whistled over her head as she staggered, marking the passing of her last bit of luck. She lurched to her feet, unwittingly smashing a Goblin in the nose with her armored knee as he sought to take advantage of her stumble. A heavy war drum boomed through the dark. The Goblins around her paused for an instant, costing one the future use of his left leg. The drum sounded again, and the Goblins surged to a higher state of furor than Lena thought possible.

She whipped her sword in quick slashing motions to fend off the raiders closest to her, all the while pounding back up the hill. The drum sounded a third time, and Lena caught a flickering light to her left. She ventured a quick glance, looking over the

Goblin horde as it trailed off down the hill behind her. A circle of torches, sputtering in the failing rain, highlighted the approach of the most massive Goblin she had ever seen. Between the distance, lack of scale, and swirling chaos around her, his height was hard to gauge, but even her quick impression put him at nearly seven feet tall. His well-muscled frame filled in his height to leave Lena with the impression that she was looking at a Troll or an exceptionally large human rather than a Goblin.

Lena batted aside an attack almost absently as she hovered on the edge of decision. The Goblin King swaggered onto the field with the confident air of a wolf approaching a wounded deer. She shot a look over her shoulder at the last remaining Ialu defending the bridge against hopeless odds. Even if she could manage to fight her way up the hill to rejoin them, there would be no chance of striking a blow against the Goblin leader from that position.

With no further hesitation, she charged back down the hill with a challenging shout, barreling straight toward the Goblin chieftain and his captains. She sliced through the few Goblins that stood in her way, though after a moment, they seemed to stand aside willingly, perhaps to save the honor of killing her for their king. She burst through the circle of torchbearers who simply stepped aside to allow her past. Ortran stood in the center of the ring facing the king with his feet planted wide. He had drawn his Ialish broadsword. With its double fullered blade nearly twice the width of most swords and terminating into a nearly rounded point, this make of weapon was nearly legendary in both its craftsmanship and its devastating cutting strength.

The Goblin King halted his forward march and stood facing Ortran with his arms folded. A Goblin captain of near equal size stood off to either side of their king, their faces seething with animosity. The Goblin horde cackled with insane glee all around the circle, but they seemed content to remain outside the ring and allow their king to strike the final blows. Lena stepped forward to stand beside Ortran, her sword held ready.

"Kind of you to join me," he offered quietly. Lena responded with only a nod and turned her attention back to the massive figures that they faced. The king extended an arm into the darkness behind. An indistinct form placed something in his hand, which he tossed underhandedly toward Lena and Ortran.

The object rolled to a stop at their feet. Lena recognized it as the head of the fellow Xedrin had sent to stir up this mess. Muddied and bloodied as it was, it was definitely the same man.

"I see you received my message." Ortran smiled wickedly.

"Hear my answer," the Goblin King spoke, his voice surprisingly articulate. A tall thin Goblin stepped forward and struggled to present his master with a truly massive blade. Styled after the Velkasian great sword, the king's weapon was far and above the finest Lena had seen amongst the Goblin horde. It must have been taken from a fallen enemy, though a weapon such as that would not be lost lightly.

"I'm surprised you have the courage to face me alone," Ortran growled. Lena could see the Ialu's blood lust beginning to rise. "Or do I need to kill all three of you at once?" He took an unconscious step forward, almost ready to spring into battle immediately. Lena knew he was baiting the king into facing him in single combat, hoping to prey on the Goblin's pride to even the odds.

"My second will face yours," the king responded with a snarl. He gestured almost distractedly, and one of the captains took a step forward. He held a wicked-looking flail in each hand, the spiked ball of each brushing the muddy ground at his feet as they dangled from a short chain fastened to a stout wooden handle held in each fist. He shook his arms to rattle the chains and smiled hungrily. Lena took a deep breath. She had never faced an opponent armed so and had little more than a vague idea on how to defend against an attack with such. She found herself longing for the shield she had abandoned earlier in the day. The other captain stepped back toward the edge of the circle and absently hefted his war hammer.

"Let us be on with it!" Ortran bellowed as he rushed forward to engage with the Goblin King. With a growl, the Goblin facing Lena lunged forward, swinging his weapons in wide arcs. His arms spun in a complex pattern, producing a swirl of heavy, jagged iron all around him. One heavy spiked ball would trace a circle only to be followed by the next, then before Lena had time to act, the first would return, screaming for her blood. He had created a wall of death around himself, making it almost impossible to approach without stepping into the path of one of his weapons.

Lena coldly admired the skill required to not only keep the weapons in motion this way but to simply avoid smashing one's self in the back of the head. As the Goblin advanced, she cautiously gave ground, studying the pattern, looking for a weakness. The Goblin smiled wickedly as he gained confidence in his tactics.

Lena darted forward to take advantage of a gap in the pattern but balked at the last moment and nearly fell over backward to avoid the spiked head of his flail. She didn't have enough reach to lunge in between his weapons to score a hit. He adjusted his motion and briefly fell into a second pattern, adjusting his momentum and throwing off Lena's calculations. She ground her teeth in frustration. She was painfully conscious of the horde of Goblins all around as they yammered and howled in delight as their masters fought. Lena was thankful that, for the moment, they seemed content to allow their chiefs to do the fighting, but she worried that if things turned poorly for the Goblin captains before the king fell, the mass of warriors that surrounded her might rush into the fight. If that happened, Lena doubted she would last more than a few seconds.

Her opponent switched back to his initial pattern, whirling his flails ever faster in an impressive and deadly display. His left hand followed neatly behind his right, eliminating any opening for her to move in, but there was a slight delay between the passing of his left weapon and the return of his right. She lunged forward, striking out to intercept the flail in his left hand, charging in to strike before the right weapon could return. The spiked head clanged off of her blade and careened away uncontrollably, but the rightmost weapon was too close behind. Lena aborted her attack and dove to the ground, narrowly avoiding catching the spiked weapon full in the chest. She rolled in the mud and struggled to her feet, gaining her balance just as her opponent was able to regain control of his flails. He resumed his whirling pattern of death.

Her breath came in ragged gasps. She had spent nearly the entire day either fighting for her life or riding like mad with death on her heels. She could not remember eating at all, and the nonstop exertion of the day was taking its toll. Her bones felt made of lead, and dizziness hovered on the edges of her consciousness. This needed to end now. Ortran and the Goblin king exchanged earth-shaking blows in a furious brawl of pure power. She felt the ground tremble beneath her feet with each colossal strike.

Lena's opponent shifted his motion and circled both weapons over his head to sweep across in a horizontal attack, one flail screaming in immediately behind the first. As Lena staggered backward to avoid the attack, her heel caught in the mud, and she toppled onto her back. With a wicked gleam in his eye, her foe swirled the weapons in one more arc, angling the spiked weapons to crash down on her where she lay. The briefest moment of delay as he countered his own momentum was all she needed to roll to one side as the spiked heads slammed into the earth where she was a moment ago, spattering her face with mud. She shot out a hand to grasp one of the chains, grabbing hold of his weapon with a strength born of desperation. He tugged on his flail, but she held fast as he spun her around on her back in the mud.

He retreated several paces, dragging Lena along behind him. He stepped forward, slinging his free weapon once in a short arc to gain momentum. Gauging his striking distance, Lena released his trapped flail and rolled toward him, lurching to her side and moving inside of the effective range of his weapon. The spiked head once again smashed into the ground behind her as she executed the only attack that was available to her, striking out with her armored elbow against his unprotected knee. With her sword hopelessly entangled beneath her body, Lena lashed out again with her fist this time, targeting her opponent's left wrist as she struggled to stand.

Bellowing with pain and frustration, the Goblin captain dropped his left weapon and lashed out, punching Lena with his empty hand, connecting with a hard uppercut. She staggered backward, the force of the blow ironically helping her to her feet. She shook her head to clear her vision and slashed blindly with her broadsword, hoping to fend the Goblin away from retrieving his fallen weapon. He cursed and stepped backward, leaving his flail in the mud.

Lena forced a toothy smile, tasting blood on her lips. Her opponent snarled and began his whirling again, making up for the loss of his second weapon with added speed. His flail spun faster and faster, its spiked head now a blur as it whirled in a deadly arc above his head. Ideally, if she were fresh, clear-headed, and on dry ground, Lena felt that she could overcome this situation; however, her circumstances now were far from ideal. Being as bone-weary as she was, the point of her sword shook with the effort of simply keeping it held aloft. Her foot slipped across the muddy, uneven ground. She spat a curse. She might very well die today, but it was not going to be this cocky son of a bitch who kills her.

She gave ground slowly, deliberately giving the impression of a cornered rabbit. Her opponent moved forward confidently, emboldened by her defensive posture. Just as Lena stepped close to the edge of the circle, she whirled around, seized a Goblin soldier by the collar, and heaved him bodily into the path of her opponent's weapon. The Goblin soldier was caught entirely off guard by this unexpected maneuver and staggered awkwardly to his death as the spiked head of the Goblin captain's flail buried itself into his body. The chain went limp in the captain's hand as all momentum was lost. Lena surged forward, leaping toward her opponent with two bounding strides. She struck his arm from his body as he raised it to defend himself and followed with a decapitating slash. His body fell into the mud with a wet splash and was still.

Ortran and the Goblin King were both a mess of bloody wounds; rivers of mud and blood covered each as they exchanged truly savage blows. Lena looked on with admiration as Ortran, who had endured the same excruciating day as herself, powered forward as if he had all the energy of a young bear. The Goblin King fought with little finesse – raining blows down upon his shorter opponent with the ruthless efficiency of a blacksmith. Ortran deflected each attack and countered with impressive speed, slashing counterattacks that would have cloven the king in two were he not quick on his feet.

The sound of squishing footsteps in the mud was the only warning she had. Lena lashed out blindly behind her with her blade, intercepting the wooden-handled war hammer of the second Goblin commander mid-swing. Her weapon spun out of her grasp as his deflected awkwardly and slipped from his fist as well. As their weapons tumbled away, she locked eyes with the Goblin. With a snarl, he lunged forward and clamped a hand down on Lena's arm as she reached for her dagger. He followed with another hand on her throat. Lena felt the bones in her wrist grind together as the dagger pitched from her useless hand. The lieutenant shifted his grip to place both hands around Lena's throat and drove her to her knees. Standing a hand taller than Lena and outweighing her by nearly a third, the Goblin already had obvious advantages in a grappling conflict. Exhausted and dazed as she was, Lena's fingers felt as if they were wrestling stone as she struggled to free herself from his grasp.

He smiled wickedly as he saw the panic begin to rise in her eyes. He pressed forward, forcing Lena onto her back on the mud. As he moved to kneel on her body, Lena fired an ineffectual right-handed punch into his ribs. He released his grip on her throat with one hand, grappling with her right arm for a moment in an attempt to immobilize it.

She shot her left hand out toward his face or throat, thrashing around to gain some tactical advantage as silver specks began to dance on the edges of her vision. She felt her right arm being pinned beneath his knee as her left hand scrambled across her opponent's face. She jammed her fingers into his mouth, grasping the lower portion of his jaw in her fist in blind desperation.

She felt his teeth clamp down onto the steel fingers of her gauntlet as she crushed the soft flesh of his mouth and twisted his jaw in her hand. Maintaining the chokehold with his left hand, he punched her with his right, though with his face firmly within Lena's gauntleted fist, he was unable to generate much power. He smashed her again while she twisted and tugged on his jaw, working her now free right hand to grapple with his weakening chokehold.

They struggled in the mud, rolling down a slight rise as Lena clamped down on her hold with all the strength she had left. She felt blows raining down on her, glancing off of her elbows and the bony portions of her skull as she twisted her grip to throw her opponent off balance, occasionally throwing in a blow of her own with her free hand.

A chorus of Goblin screams broke the night. Lena's opponent instantly abandoned all attempts to injure her and thrashed his body, heaving against her grasp in a desperate attempt to escape. Her fingers slipped as he lurched to his feet, leaving Lena with a handful of bloody teeth. He fought to his feet and bolted away into the night. Lena rolled to her side and scrambled to her sword, where it lay in the mud. Ortran knelt on the ground beside the Goblin King's headless corpse, the chief's massive blade having pierced the Ialu directly through the middle. The Goblin horde was scattering into the dark, shrieking in abject horror at their loss, running heedlessly in all directions, oblivious to anything and anyone around them. Within moments no living Goblin inhabited the field. Lena grabbed her sword from the mud and scrambled on her hands and knees to Ortran's side as he pitched over into the mud. He had lost his helm in the fray, and a gash across his scalp bled freely into his left eye. He looked up at Lena as she crouched over him.

"I got the bastard," he proclaimed. A weak cough shook his body, producing a pained wince. "He was a big one."

"I think the plan worked; they are scattering." Lena shot a look over her shoulder to confirm her statement. The rain had slowed to a mere drizzle, and a few of the torches abandoned by the Goblins lay sputtering in the mud. She could see movement at the top of the hill by the bridge. She waved her arm to gain their attention.

"Bunch of cowards. Damn Goblins..." He fell into another fit of painful coughing.

"Just hold still." Lena paused to examine his wound. The Goblin's massive sword had forced its way between the armor plate protecting Ortran's chest and a plate over his abdomen. She could see runes inscribed along the blade's surface as they slowly filled with the Ialu's lifeblood. The sword had been run completely through his body to exit by the complementary seam across his back. She was shocked that he was still breathing. "Pevma might be able to patch you up."

"No need to lie to me."

"Vochny! Pevma!" Lena shouted. She could hear footsteps splashing through the mud as her fellows approached.

"Miss Sullivan..." Ortran stammered. His eyes rolled around in his head for a moment, and Lena feared he was lost. Vochny skidded to a halt beside her, his muddied armor a bloody mess. He ascertained his captain's injuries with a glance. Pevma arrived a moment later, staggering visibly as she dropped to her knees beside the dying Ialu. Lena nodded toward the blade protruding from Ortran's belly. Pevma shook her head silently. Vochny took a breath as if to speak but fell silent as Ortran waved his words away. His breath grated unevenly in his throat, making a wet, raspy gurgle.

He motioned for Lena and Vochny to lean closer. He dabbed the tip of his forefinger in the spring of blood pouring from his body and drew a symbol first on Vochny's armored chest plate and then upon Lena's. She sat up unconsciously, confused. Vochny's eyes grew wide as he took in the image scrawled on their armor. Ortran's hand fell to the mud as he breathed his last. After a moment, Vochny spoke.

"Miss Sullivan," he began. "You have earned an Ialish campaign tattoo. It is an honor not commonly bestowed outside of our people, but it is yours if you would have it."

"I would be honored," she answered, struggling to her feet.

"Let us leave this place," Vochny stated. "I would be deeply disappointed if the Goblins were overly quick to choose a new king."

CHAPTER NINE

Lena nodded to the serving boy as he refilled her teapot. Her stomach rumbled slightly in anticipation of taking lunch, but she had promised to wait for her companions, and she kept her promises. Usually. If the serving boy returned before her companions arrived, she would put in an order for an appetizer, though. No one could fault her for that. At least it was a lovely day to be kept waiting. The outdoor café that the professor had recommended, the Five Ponies, commanded a lovely view of one of Nephron's many open squares.

She had been playfully warned not to ask the reason for the establishment's namesake for fear of receiving a long-winded and rather anticlimactic explanation. However, if the professor was significantly tardy for lunch today (though at this point in their acquaintance, she had resigned to his being *somewhat* late as a rule), as a form of light chastisement, she would deliberately ask the host that very question once the professor had settled himself.

Thin white clouds drifted lazily above in an unhurried fashion, setting themselves against the deep blue sky as if they were pretending that they didn't know they were spectacular, and any compliments as such would be met with a feigned startled shrug. She had been surprised at how dry the air in the city was, but as fortune would have it, Ialu do very much enjoy discussing geography and the weather. (Or was it misfortune?) Nephron was nestled in a narrow valley between two separate mountain ranges. The Anghar Mountains loomed to the west, and the Paramian Mountains from which she had recently descended, stood to the east. The swath of dead prairie known only as the Wasteland stretched to the north with those two mountain ranges on either side. The Wasteland opened up from its most narrow point here just beyond the walls of Nephron to a vast expanse of dead land far to the north where it slowly faded into the thick, untamed forests of what was once the kingdom of Haveria.

After arriving in town nearly a week ago, she had expected the place to have been soaked through. However, she had learned in a somewhat roundabout fashion that the mountains to either side of Nephron, and also, therefore, the wasteland, effectively blocked most of the rainfall, leaving Nephron and the dead land to the north quite dry for most of the year. Lena shuddered unconsciously as her thoughts drifted back to those blood-soaked mountains.

She knew that she was lucky to be alive. Why Zadarsti (the Ialish god of luck) had chosen to spare her over the sixteen Ialish soldiers who had breathed their last along that mountain pass was a mystery. Lena didn't truly believe in luck or in the gods (of any culture), but the guilt she felt in surviving the horrific ordeal when so many others did not was definitely real. She closed her eyes but only saw the bloody, lifeless face of young Hagen, who had been brave enough to admit his fear but now would never be able to regale a tavern with stories of fierce battle. She looked back across the square at the warm sandstone buildings of the city and watched the people passing by.

While Nephron was known worldwide as a stronghold of the Ialu, it was certainly still inhabited by all other peoples as well. A mixed group of humans, Ialu and C'thûn flowed by laughing carelessly; likely, none of them have ever looked death in the eye. She had been warned by Instructor Narziim in the Pheldian Academy to be wary of becoming emotionally detached from the rest of society. It was easy to fall into the trap of either feeling superior to or simply apart from those who had never fought, those who had never faced death. Narziim had pounded a philosophy into his students' heads that the soul of the warrior was servitude. The only reason to fight was to protect yourself or defend those who could not protect themselves. If a person never had to bleed in the field or watch their friends die in the mud, then you, as a warrior, were doing your job. She shook the darkness from her mind and sipped her tea, striving to enjoy the warm afternoon sun.

"Lena!" Resaka waved as he approached, nodding to the serving boy as he sat.

"Burkus let you off work for the day?" Lena teased. Whatever business Burkus had with the Red Hand leadership, it had immediately consumed him upon arrival in Nephron, and therefore Resaka's time was mostly spent as well.

"Here in the heart of Ialu warrior country, Mister Burkus has finally decided that he feels safe enough to venture out of doors without my esteemed protection." Resaka laughed. Nephron was a notoriously law-abiding city. The town guard was somewhat overfunded and overstaffed and pursued their jobs with pride and zeal. The chief constable was a human named Horkun Cobb, and the locals joked that his last name stood for **C**ount **O**n **B**eing **B**usted. In her short time in Nephron, however, Lena had already heard several stories about the enthusiasm for policing being taken too far on occasion. If one was a member of a less esteemed class by the misfortune of blood or station, then the reputation of Nephron's town guard took on an entirely different meaning.

However, Lena had the privilege of being human, and as a warrior herself, she would automatically receive preferential treatment. It irked her to the bone. If she witnessed a guardsman harassing an Azrak for no good reason (as guardsmen were likely to do in any city), she knew perfectly well that she would step in, and things might get ugly. She wasn't sure what it said about her that a part of her looked forward to such an encounter.

"How's the leg?" she asked him.

"Heald up quite nicely, courtesy of the deep pockets of our hosts." Resaka unconsciously massaged his thigh. He had taken multiple wounds to his leg, and once the passion of battle had passed, he had barely been able to stand much less walk.

"That's the same gap in your guard that Master Garis warned you about," she chided. "You fight shorter opponents downhill again, and you might not make it home next time."

"Yeah, yeah," he admitted begrudgingly. "Old habits."

"Practice your Floating Lotus form."

"You sound just like him."

"Thank you for the compliment." She pointed at him for emphasis. "I mean it. Practice. That. Form. The next time I see you, you had better be floating lotuses in your sleep."

"So, you *do* plan to see me again," Resaka commented.

"Don't start with that," She sighed. "I told you. Pevma and I are back with the wagon train and off to Roth tomorrow."

"Mister Reyhas pays pretty well," Resaka admitted. "I had a beer with Kar and Shaab yesterday after they arrived. Shaab is still disappointed he didn't get his rematch, by the way," Resaka teased with a twinkle in his eye.

"Well, from what I hear, the road north along the edge of the mountains is pretty boring," Lena commented. Not much lived along the edges of the Wasteland, and consequently, there was little reason to take to banditry if there was no one to steal from. "Plenty of time for archery practice."

"Well, Kar still has a wild hair to go out into the waste looking for runestones and lost cities." Resaka shook his head. "Talk him out of it if you can."

"He's a grown boy. He can do whatever he wants." Lena shrugged.

"Yeah, but he owes me fifty silver, and he can't pay if he's dead." Resaka thanked the serving boy as another teacup arrived. "What?" Resaka responded to Lena's arched eyebrow. "Kar is a lousy card player; I don't know what else to say." Lena chuckled. She caught sight of the professor as he peered into the bright sun from the shadowy café interior. She stood and waved him over.

"Miss Sullivan, Mister Devaash, how good to see you both." He smiled genuinely and shook each of their hands excessively as he sat.

"Thank you for joining us, Professor. I know you have been busy with your book."

"I am pleased to be able to spend an afternoon with such fine folks as yourselves." Durwynn practically beamed. "Tea? How very civilized of you, Miss Sullivan. I should say that a lovely afternoon such as this calls for wine at the very least, would you not agree?" Without waiting for any such agreement, the professor summoned the serving boy and made his request, calling for an unfamiliar Ialish varietal. "I trust red is acceptable?" he asked as an afterthought.

Their conversation dwelt mainly upon the fine points of Ialish cuisine (which they enjoyed rather universally) and the health of each of the few survivors of their ordeal. All had been healed of their physical wounds, courtesy of the Ialish healers. Even Pevma, who had initially been viewed with a sour eye by the Red Hand mages, received exceptional care once her contributions to their cause had been made clear. Vochny had been her staunch supporter and quite firmly chastised the attendant for his poor attitude. Of the other soldiers, only Urzbek, Alcher, and Betov remained. All three were in good health and had begun to recruit new soldiers for a unit under Vochny's command as a newly promoted captain. If the Ialish shaman had been surprised to see Lena when she arrived to receive her campaign tattoo along with the Ialish soldiers, then he hid it well. After the ritual marking, the boys had insisted that large amounts of whiskey *must* be consumed, and Lena scarcely remembered returning to her room that night. The following morning was a brutal reminder of the dangers of going out for a drink with Ialish soldiers.

"And how is our young friend Maco?" Lena asked.

"Ahh. Maco." The professor took an overlong sip from his wine and absently fiddled with a morsel of potato on his plate. "I believe he has some challenges ahead."

"I see." Lena hid a smile behind her wine. She hadn't laid an eye on the young man since the day they had staggered into Nephron, but secondhand reports had painted quite a picture.

"May I be candid with you two?" the professor asked, receiving a nod from his two table companions. "I don't think that Maco fully appreciates the sacrifices that were made on our journey through the mountains, nor do I think he understands why they were made."

"He's a little shit who thinks he's more important than anyone else and assumes all those men died just to save *him*," Resaka mumbled into this own wine.

"I suppose that's another way of putting it," the professor conceded. "In any case, a lesson in humility is on the near horizon for him. He has no savvy for politics, and now that Ortran is gone, no allies." The professor sighed. "The leadership of the *Servé Ruche* will make of him what they will."

"They are going to eat him for lunch, aren't they?" Lena asked.

"More like an appetizer," the professor answered with a twinkling eye. "The contract that bears his name carries importance to all his people. It is larger than he himself, or even the esteemed name he carries. At some point, he will learn that."

"Or he won't," Lena added.

"Perhaps not," the professor admitted. "For some, life lessons are difficult to absorb."

"How is Vochny doing with his new unit?" Resaka asked. "He got promoted or something, right?"

"I like Vochny," the professor said evasively.

"That well?" Lena asked. The professor ventured a look over each shoulder in what was a solid attempt at causal subtlety, but the gesture was an almost universal sign that something delicate was about to be spoken.

"Vochny is going to have some troubles," the professor answered quietly. "The *Servé Ruche* has a certain... political perspective." He leaned forward and dropped his voice even softer. "Ortran, rest his soul, is receiving all the glory for winning the mine back for the people, and Vochny is receiving all of the ire for involving people who are not Ialu."

"Does my campaign honor cause problems for him?" Lena asked. "If I thought it was going to be an issue…"

"It was Ortran's wish," Durwynn answered. "It was the right thing to do – to honor the sacrifices of those fallen soldiers and the dying wish of their captain." He paused. "But, yes, sadly, it is an issue. The Red Hand has a strongly nationalist view, and to have non-Ialu, such as yourself and Pevma, included in the official accounting of the tale is a thorn in their side. And Vochny is paying for it."

"That's bullshit." Lena tapped her fist on the table with ire.

"That's politics."

"Same thing," Resaka suggested.

"True," the professor agreed. "If we were dealing with a more progressive clan, like the Black Hammer, then this would be a complete non-issue. Both Lena and even Pevma would have permanent standing invitations to any gatherings and clan functions. They would be welcomed as kin."

"So, what happens to Vochny?" Resaka followed.

"To captain a private company, Vochny must find twenty volunteers. If he cannot fill his quota, he and the others will be separated and assigned to larger units. His commanders would see to it that he is never promoted or given the opportunity to distinguish himself."

"Why doesn't he quit then? Join a reasonable clan?" Lena asked. She found herself growing deeply angry at the way Vochny would be treated.

"I'm afraid clan affiliation is for life," the professor sighed. "There is no other option."

"I hate to say it, but I'm almost sorry to be associated with them," Lena admitted. When she had taken part in the ritual marking, she had only thoughts for the men who had died bravely in the mud to save their kindred. The honor of inclusivity, the shared bond of soldiers in the field, was her only consideration. The darker aspects of politics and nationalism were unknown to her.

"Well, my friend, rest at ease." The professor put a hand on her forearm. "By Ialish tradition, the mark you bear knows no clan. If multiple clans were present in those mountains, they would all bear the same mark. It proclaims only that you fought alongside Ialu soldiers with distinction and honor. It may serve you well in the future." Lena nodded in assent. Knowing that it did not tie her to any clan assuaged the distaste she felt, but the anger at how Vochny would fare as a result still stung.

"You watch yourself." Lena pointed a Resaka. He responded with a lifted eyebrow. "Your Burkus fellow is still dealing with these characters." He raised his hands in resignation.

"The man pays. Am I supposed to tell him who he should be doing business with?"

"You have a choice," she stated.

"If life has taught me anything, and arguably it hasn't..." Resaka began. Lena bit off a premature agreement out of respect for her friend. "But if it *has*..." he went on. "It's that everyone everywhere is awful," Resaka proclaimed. "If I turn down work from anyone who isn't a saint, then I'm never going to work. Nobody has perfectly pure motives. Nobody who needs to employ a swordsman anyway." Resaka took a sip of his wine.

"You could always go back to piracy," Lena suggested with a wry grin.

"Might be more respectable," Resaka admitted with a laugh. "So, listen, you two. I am profoundly grateful to have both of you in my life and would consider it a personal favor if you allow me to buy our lunch today."

"Nonsense boy, I won't hear of it." The professor nearly scowled at the C'thûn. "And you will respect the wishes of your elders without complaint," He finished.

"Very well." Resaka bowed his head in defeat. "However, I still owe this young lady a whiskey, and it seems that tonight is my final chance. If I am denied this afternoon, allow me the honor of buying you both a round tonight. Say, sunset at the Twisted Serpent?"

"I would be honored, my friend," the professor stated solemnly.

"Then I must bid you a temporary farewell, and I look forward to seeing you both tonight." Resaka rose from his seat and made an exaggerated bow.

"I'll see you tonight, but one condition," Lena stated.

"Name it."

"No sappy, long goodbye crap," she chided with a grin. "You know I hate that."

"Of course." Resaka looked genuinely abashed, though Lena knew it was an act. "I'll settle for a see you later."

"Get out of here." She laughed. Resaka performed another theatrical bow and removed himself from the patio.

"Well, my dear…" the professor started. "And I say 'my dear' because you have become dear to me. I won't apologize." He winked at her with his eyes twinkling.

"I'll allow it," she conceded.

"I *do* wish you luck."

"Oh, I don't think this next job requires much luck," Lena answered. "All reports I have heard suggest the road north is fraught with boredom."

"I rather mean luck in finding your peace."

"Peace?" Lena asked. "With what?"

"I don't know," the professor said solemnly. "But I suspect you do." He patted her forearm as he rose. "I will attend to the bill, and I look forward to raising another glass with you and Mister Devaash tonight. Be well, my dear." The professor bowed his head and ambled casually toward the café's interior, fumbling about with his coin purse. Lena sat quietly for a moment and savored the last bit of her wine. She had rather enjoyed Nephron despite its numerous failings. Perhaps a return trip someday was in order. But, for now, Lena found herself looking forward to what the city of Roth had to offer.

THANKS

Thank you for reading my book. Rise of the Red Hand is a prequel to the full-length novel Storm Cloud Rising, the first volume of the Storm Cloud series. If you enjoyed reading this and would be interested in more, I encourage you to visit my website www.jasonlancour.com, where, if you're feeling particularly adventurous, you can sign up for my newsletter. Or, if perhaps you're more into the social media thing, I maintain (to varying degrees) a profile on some of the popular platforms using the handle jasonlancourauthor. In either place, you'll be able to receive updates about future work, writing related news, inside info, idle ramblings, and perhaps a map or two.

Jason Lancour

LENA WILL RETURN

IN

STORM CLOUD RISING

No prophecy. No Chosen One. No greatest hero of all time.

The fate of the world does not hang in the balance.

A group of mercenaries is hired for what was *supposed* to be an easy assignment. Get in. Get out. Get paid. But like most things in life, nothing is as easy as it seems. In a world rich with history, meticulously engineered laws of magic, unique cultures and peoples (as well as the occasional whiskey joint), the "private contractors" soon find their already varied motivations and priorities shifting. What started out as a simple job spirals out of control into a struggle for survival in the midst of a plot that is bigger – much bigger – than any of them could ever have anticipated. Blood will be spilled, confidences broken, and a fair bit of whiskey consumed. Not everyone is who they seem, and no one seems in control.

This is only the beginning…

Made in the USA
Monee, IL
28 March 2022

93661128R00080